THE TAKEDOWN

MIDDLE SCHOOL MAYHEM SERIES: BOOK SIX

C.T. WALSH

Publisher's Cataloging-in-Publication Data

provided by Five Rainbows Cataloging Services

Names: Walsh, C.T., author.

Title: The takedown / C.T. Walsh.

Description: Bohemia, NY : Farcical Press, 2020. | Series: Middle school mayhem, bk. 6. | Summary: Austin and Principal Buthaire have an epic showdown that will result in one of them leaving Cherry Avenue Middle School forever. | Audience: Grades 5 & up. | Also available in ebook and audiobook formats.

Identifiers: ISBN 978-1-950826-05-6 (paperback)

Subjects: LCSH: Bildungsromans. | Youth protest movements--Juvenile fiction. | CYAC: Middle school students--Fiction. | Middle schools--Fiction. | School principals--Fiction. | Humorous stories. | BISAC: JUVENILE FICTION / Social Themes / Adolescence & Coming of Age. | JUVENILE FICTION / School & Education. | JUVENILE FICTION / Humorous Stories. | JUVENILE FICTION / Boys & Men.

Classification: LCC PZ7.1.W35 Tak 2019 (print) | LCC PZ7.1.W35 (ebook) | DDC [Fic]--dc23.

COVER CREDITS

Cover design by Books Covered
Cover photographs © Shutterstock
Cover illustrations by Maeve Norton

For my Family

Thank you for all of your support

1

Everybody loves an underdog. Well, except for the overdogs. Is that even a word? If not, it should be. At Cherry Avenue Middle School, home of the ferocious Gophers, I was that beloved underdog. And I had three overdogs who loved stealing my bone and pooping on my front lawn. I mean, not literally. Well, one of them was my butt-chinned brother, Derek, and he set off a lot of bags of flaming poo on our front lawn, but they weren't always directed at me. Sometimes, they were in protest of something my parents had done. It was a strange way to protest, but my brother isn't exactly known for his sophistication. But he gets away with more than me because he has the family butt chin and I don't. Nobody said life was fair, kids.

Anyway, it was the first day back at school after the Medieval Renaissance fair, a fabulous place where I had made a handful of overdogs incredibly unhappy. I walked off the bus and into school half expecting the war with Principal Butt Hair (a term of endearment for our less-than likable Principal Buthaire), no, fully expecting, the war to continue. I wasn't expecting a Kung-Fu kick to the face right on the spot, but I hid in the shadows like a ninja just in case. I ducked behind the hulking Nick DeRozan, did a dive roll behind a bench, nearly concussed myself, and popped up behind one of the dogwood trees in the Atrium. Not only is it a weird name for a tree, but they were pretty thin and not overly helpful in providing ninja shade.

Thankfully, I made it to my Advisory class undetected. My buddy, Just Charles sat next to me. I know it's a strange nickname, but he kind of gave it to himself. People called him Charlie or Chuck so many times and he hated it. He would yell, "My name is just Charles!" It kinda stuck.

It didn't take long for Butt Hair to take his first shot at me. The Speaker of Doom crackled in the corner of the classroom. Just Charles looked at me. I smiled and stood up.

"That's my cue," I said.

Mrs. Callahan was busy writing something down. She didn't look up. "Please sit...oh, Austin, Mrs. Murphy already told me that you were getting called down."

And right on cue, Mrs. Murphy whined, "Austin Davenport to the principal's office for the thousandth time. And Sophie Rodriguez."

Say what? Sophie was my girlfriend. She never got in trouble, although she was my partner in the Medieval Renaissance quest, and she beat Emperor Buthaire just as badly as I did, if not more.

I walked as quickly as I could. I wanted to beat Sophie there. She would need my support. I figured she was in shell shock. I sat in the main office, waiting for her to show up so we could receive our first couple's detention from Prince Butt Hair. I'm a real romantic. The office was bustling with activity even more than usual. I didn't chart traffic patterns or anything, but when you're there as much as I was, you get a good feel for things. I furrowed my brow as I looked into the small office next to The Butt Crack, Principal Buthaire's office, to see a woman I didn't recognize. She was unpacking boxes.

The door squeaked open and Sophie walked in. Even though we were in the principal's office and yelling was likely to ensue shortly, I was still happy to see her. She forced a smile and slumped down into the seat next to me.

"Hey," I said.

Sophie took a deep breath. "Is this how it feels every time?"

"The sense of dread and extreme unfairness? Yep. And enjoy this one, because each one gets worse."

"Ugh," she said, putting her face in her hands.

"Is this your first time in the principal's office, ever?" I asked, somewhat amused.

"Yes. My parents are gonna be so happy. How many is this for you?"

"Lost count. I should be writing it all down so I could tell the planet's youth all about it, though. I think my story would be a global phenomenon."

"Yeah, I think you're right." Sophie looked into the office next to Principal Buthaire's and asked, "Who is that?"

"Probably a new office manager or something. Prince Butt Hair fires them like he changes his underwear."

"Never?"

I laughed and then turned it into a cough as Principal Buthaire emerged from The Butt Crack. His eyes bored into me. He didn't even say anything. He just pointed at me with two fingers and then down at the floor in front of him. Sophie and I stood up and walked over to his office. Even though I had been through it a hundred times, my pulse still pounded throughout my body.

Principal Buthaire lowered himself slowly into the chair

and then straightened his stapler and tie. He stared at us for a minute before speaking. "Do you know why you're here?"

"Because you ordered us to be?" I asked.

Principal Butt Hair shook his head slowly. "You are like an annoying little fly, Misterrrr Davenport. Buzzing, buzzing, buzzing in your ear. You try to swat it, but miss. You roll up a magazine or grab a fly swatter and take a few more swings. It's annoying when you keep missing, because they're pesky little creatures and they can make you look like a fool, but it's oh so satisfying when you finally connect and squash that annoying little fly. I take particular pleasure in watching it twitch before it takes its last breath."

I looked at Sophie. She was normally Wonder Woman under pressure, but her face was pale. She probably never understood the extent of how much of an idiot Principal Buthaire was. I've been known to exaggerate a thing or two, so maybe my friends didn't fully believe me when I told them all of my stories.

My eyes returned to Prince Butt Hair. "That's dark, sir."

"It's the circle of life. That's how the food chain works."

I wasn't a fly expert by any means, but I am a science genius, so I was pretty certain he was wrong, but I had learned over time that certain battles weren't worth fighting. I had enough big Butt Hair battles to deal with.

"Ms. Rodriguez, I hope this does not become a habit with you. I fear that if you continue to keep the same company, it will be." He stared at me as his voice shook with anger, "Bad influences will drag you down." Principal Buthaire looked back at Sophie. "I was particularly hurt by the arrow you shot at me during the Renaissance Fair. And for that, you get detention."

"That's not fair," I said. "It wasn't a school event."

Sophie said, "And it was rubber and it only hit your goblet."

"That's all well and good, but now you both get detention for arguing with your principal."

"That's not fair," Sophie said, stupefied.

"We were arguing because you were wrong," I said.

"The detention stands." Principal Buthaire reached into the inner pocket of his suit jacket and pulled out his best (and only) friend, his detention pad. He tore off two slips and handed them to us. "I'm in a good mood today. Hurry to class before you're late."

I stood up, ready to sprint out of there before he changed his mind, but Sophie appeared frozen in her seat.

"Soph, time to go. Like, now," I said.

Sophie shook her head and stood up. I gently prodded her out of the office. I shut the door behind me, as we left to make sure he couldn't shout more detentions out at us from his chair.

The woman from the office next door stared at us as I ushered Sophie out of the office.

"It really gets worse than this?" Sophie asked.

"Pretty much every time. That was actually a good one, though. Definitely savor it. I wonder why the heck he was in a good mood after the Renaissance Fair?" What was I missing? I didn't even know it was possible for him to be in a good mood.

As I was getting my binder for English class, Just Charles and Cheryl Van Snoogle-Something walked by within a larger crowd of kids, all seemingly going in the same direction. They had been partners at the Medieval Renaissance fair quest that we all participated in. I wondered if there was a budding romance at hand. Just Charles was just like me, unsure why a girl like Cheryl was actually interested in him.

I was the Cherry Avenue Gopher poster boy for having a girlfriend 'out of my league' with Sophie.

"What are you doing?" Just Charles asked, stopping beside me.

"Getting my books for class. What are you doing? Where is everyone going?"

"There's no class," Cheryl said. "There's an assembly."

Just Charles said, "Oh, yeah. You missed the morning announcements. Again. What did Butt Hair want?"

"To harass me. I love assemblies."

Sammie walked up and stopped to join the group. She was one of my besties, having grown up next door to me.

"Any idea what it is?" Cheryl asked.

"Beats me," Just Charles said. "The Speaker of Doom didn't say."

Sammie said cheerily, "I hope it's something cool."

"Like what?" Cheryl asked.

"I don't know. Maybe an author."

"Like who?"

"C.T. Walsh. That guy is awesome," Sammie said.

"Agreed. And so handsome," Cheryl said.

"Meh," Sammie said, shrugging.

Guys don't like talking about how handsome other guys are, no matter how cool C.T. Walsh was, and it was an off-the-charts level of cool. I hoped to meet him at Comic-Con during the summer. My dad said he would take us. But I had to change the subject. "Anybody seen Randy yet?"

"Thankfully, no," Just Charles said.

"I haven't, either," Sammie said, but she didn't appear to be as thankful as Charles. She had a crush on Randy last year and I wasn't sure if she was completely over it. Even though her taste in authors was superb, her taste in boys was the exact opposite.

"Slow down," I said, "so we don't have to see him. He's up front. Can't you see his big head up there?"

I looked across the Atrium. Through the crowd of assembly-goers, I could see two men installing some sort of video screen or scoreboard.

"What the heck is that?" I asked.

"Maybe it's so we can play video games between classes," Just Charles said, laughing.

"Yeah, right. It's more likely that Butt Hair streams videos of me getting yelled at. Sophie joined me in that fun endeavor this morning."

"I heard," Just Charles said. He turned to Sophie. "Sorry to hear."

Sophie just shrugged. "I just feel bad that Austin has to deal with that every week. He's such a jerk and so unfair."

"Who, Butt Hair?" Sammie asked, chuckling. "Not him." She rolled her eyes.

As we filed into the auditorium, I searched for signs of what was planned. I didn't see any handsome or not-so-handsome authors. No police officers or zoo animals. The assembly was a giant mystery.

Sophie and Ben joined our group as we grabbed seats in the middle of the auditorium. Most of our crew were nerds, but even we knew that it wasn't cool to sit too close up front. I sat down next to Sophie and settled in. Out of the corner of my eye, I saw Randy climbing over people in the row ahead of us. He stopped a few seats from us. He looked down at the dude in front of him and said, "You're in my seat."

The kid stood up quickly and scooted out of the row. Randy sat down. I hadn't realized it at first, but Regan was in the seat next to him. I wondered what was going on with the two of them after things ended, well, badly for them at the Renaissance Fair.

"Hey," he said to Regan with his fake smile.

She ignored him.

"You still mad at me?"

"You're good," Regan spat.

Randy smiled and said, "Thanks!" And then realized it wasn't actually a compliment. "How many times can I say it? I'm sorry."

"Don't care." Regan said icily and turned her body away from him.

Randy stared at me and said, "What're you looking at, Davenfart?"

"A train wreck," I said. I couldn't help myself, so I added, "Now you know how it feels to be treated like garbage."

"Shut your face, Davenfart," Randy said, his face red. He turned away with a huff.

Thankfully, the lights flickered and Principal Buthaire walked out onto the stage, a microphone in his hand. He was strutting his stuff like a dumb peacock like I hadn't just taken him down at the Renaissance Fair. The place was dead silent, but based on the look on his face, you would think that he was getting a standing ovation. It was concerning. It was never a good sign when Butt Hair was happy. It meant he was going to make the rest of us unhappy.

"Good morning, Gophers!"

The crowd responded with a few grunts. Gary Larkin threw out a fake fart. Or maybe it was real. He was that good.

Prince Butt Hair continued, "I have been working on a secret project that has finally come to fruition."

Just Charles leaned toward me and asked, "What, is he planting apple trees?"

"I just completed a global search for my protege and I am pleased, no, overjoyed, to introduce you to her."

A woman walked out to the stage, smiling. She was well dressed and proper. It was the same woman from the main office earlier.

Sophie whispered to me, "She looks nice. Maybe she won't be so bad."

"You think Butt Hair's protege is going to be nice? Who do you know that Butt Hair likes that is actually nice?"

"We can hope."

"Hope is a dangerous strategy when it comes to Cherry Avenue Middle School. I think our motto is actually, 'we crush children's hopes and dreams.'"

Sophie elbowed me with a smile.

Principal Buthaire continued his introduction. "Ms. Anne Pierre comes from the prestigious Academy of Worcester, a school with students much better than this one. We're lucky to have her. Let me read you her bio. It's quite impressive." He pulled out a piece of paper from his suit jacket as Ms. Pierre stood beside him, smiling at the crowd. "Ah, here we are." Principal Buthaire looked at Ms. Pierre and smiled. He read, "Ms. Pierre completed her teacher training at the Harvard Graduate School of Education. She is currently writing her PhD dissertation on Classroom Management and Student Behavior. She has a blessed balance of a nurturing spirit with firm discipline. She enjoys evening strolls with her dog, Monty, and moulding the minds of today's youth and tomorrow's leaders."

"Who is she, the Mary Poppins of Vice Principals?" Sophie asked.

Principal Buthaire put the paper away and said, "She is, without a doubt, going to shape our pedagogy for years to come here at Cherry Avenue Middle School."

"Pedawhoey?" Just Charles whispered.

"I thought he said something about petting a goat. I'm lost," I said with a shrug.

"Please give her a warm Gopher greeting. She's our new Vice Principal, Ms. Anne Pierre!"

There were more claps and cheers than I thought there would be, but I guess there was some hope that she would be an improvement over Principal Buthaire. She did sound like the Mary Poppins of Principaling.

"I don't want to overwhelm Ms. Pierre on her first day. I'll just ask her to give us a few words to describe what she wants to see during her time here."

"Pain," she said, pounding her fist into her palm, laughing maniacally. "Just kidding. I want to see the wonderful smiles of all these sweet children, as their brains expand and their friendships flourish."

2

Nobody knew what to make of Ms. Pierre. She seemed qualified. She certainly smiled more than Principal Buthaire, but she also seemed to be a bit unpredictable. The one quality I appreciated in Prince Butt hair was his predictability. True, he was predictably heinous, but at least I knew what to expect.

I sat at my science lab table with Sophie. It was a big day in seventh grade science. It was frog dissection day. Most kids loved it. Some kids hated it. I was actually pretty excited. Sophie? Not as excited. She wasn't a prissy kind of girl, but finding enjoyment from gutting a dead frog is not on the top of most people's lists.

"You're doing this," Sophie said.

I adjusted my goggles and slipped on a pair of latex gloves. Sophie handed me the scalpel. "Should we name him?" I asked.

"No. Definitely not."

"Aww, come on. You don't like Kermie?"

"If you name him Kermie, we're gonna have a serious problem, mister."

I looked up at Sophie. She had the same fire in her eyes when she held the bow and arrow at the Medieval Renaissance Fair. "Just kidding," I said, and looked back at the frog I had pinned to the silver tray.

"The first thing we're supposed to do is an incision down the midline of the abdomen."

I leaned in and lined the scalpel up on the frog's midline, right under its neck. I pressed down on the blade with my finger.

"The skin is tougher than I thought. The worm was easier."

"Mmm, hmm," Sophie said, seemingly trying not to puke. She had her nose and mouth tucked into her shirt.

I pressed down harder on the scalpel. I felt the blade starting to slice into the frog's skin.

"She's here," Sophie said.

"Who's here?"

"Mrs. Pierre."

I pressed down on the scalpel and the blade sliced through the skin with a pop. At least I thought it was a pop until I looked up to see Kermie's eyeball soaring across the lab.

"Oh, God. No!" I yelled. "Mrs. Pierre, look out!"

In hindsight, it was the wrong thing to do. Instead of allowing the slimy eyeball of the dead frog I was dissecting to perhaps hit her in the back of the head or perhaps not hit her at all, I called her attention to the fact that my frog's eyeball was heading toward her. And instead of the back of her head, it was now tearing through the air like a meteor right toward her face.

Ms. Pierre calmly turned in my direction as she assessed the situation. She reached her hand up and snatched the eyeball out of the air like an All-Star shortstop. The class froze, not sure what her response would be. Even Mr. Gifford looked like he might need a diaper.

Ms. Pierre tossed the frog's eyeball up into the air and caught it again like it was a baseball and not a disgusting and slimy reptilious ocular sphere. She casually strolled over to Sophie and me, her eyes locked on mine.

"Good afternoon, Mrs. Pierre," I said, nervously. I put the scalpel down as I wasn't sure if she would try to disarm me with some crazy Kung-Fu move or something. "I'm really sorry about that. It just popped out."

"It's Ms. Not Mrs."

I looked at her, confused. She seemed to take more offense that I called her by the wrong title than by nearly dismembering her with a creepy reptile eyeball.

She looked at me and said, "It's socially ambiguous and mysterious."

"Okay. I see how that would be beneficial."

"Very. And what's your name?" she asked me.

I was about to say something, anything but my own name, like something cool. I was thinking Jack Tucker or something tough, like Tito. And she'd ask, "Do you have a last name, Tito?" And I'd say, "Nah. Just call me Tito."

But Ditzy Dayna had to go and ruin it. It was the first time she ever got my name right. "He's Austin Davenport!"

"It's a pleasure to make your acquaintance, Misterrrr Davenport." She held the 'r' like Principal Butt Hair did when he was mad. "I won't waste any of your time getting to know you now. Principal Buthaire told me we'll have plenty of time for that. Sorry I missed you this morning."

I didn't know how to respond, so I just stood there staring at her like an idiot.

Ms. Pierre flipped Kermie's eyeball at me. Instinctively, I grabbed it. My hand gripped the eyeball with a gooey squish.

"Enjoy." She smiled, as if that somehow made it less weird.

"Nice work, Froggiefart," Randy called out.

I rushed around our lab table to quickly wash my hands.

Thankfully, everyone was so weirded out by Ms. Pierre that they didn't make any comments about how disgusting it was. And it was.

Ms. Pierre continued without missing a beat. "And you must be Miss Rodriguez."

"I am. It's nice to meet you, Ms. Pierre."

"That's a colorful shirt, Miss Rodriguez," Ms. Pierre said.

"Oh, thank you."

"It wasn't a compliment, dear."

"Oh," Sophie said, confused.

I looked up and down at Ms. Pierre. She wore a gray pants suit with a black blouse and shoes. Her necklace was silver and simple. And then it all made sense. She was the female version of Butt Hair. She was just missing the mustache. And for that, I was thankful. The same could not be said for half of the cafeteria staff, which was probably why we lead the state in hairy hamburgers.

"Well, have a fabulous day, everyone!" Ms. Pierre said with a wave. She patted me on the shoulder and slyly wiped her eyeballed palm on my shirt.

Sophie and I looked at each other, eyes bulging. She was going to be a tough one. Maybe even tougher than Butt Hair. And I didn't even want to think about the prospect of the two of them working together.

~

IT WAS TIME FOR MY COUPLES' detention with Sophie. It might've stunk for her, but I was so used to detention without her that having her was a treat. It was like visiting day in prison, not that I have any experience with that, although maybe in the future. Who knows how Derek is going to turn out? Although, I'm sure some idiot judge would get his case and let him off with a warning just because he has a butt chin.

Sophie sat next to me. Artie Lungren, Sarah Vessey, Gary Larkin, and Jason Tannen were also scattered around the classroom.

I looked over at Sophie and said, "Welcome to my life. You never get used to it. This is the worst place on earth." I may have been exaggerating.

"We just get to do our homework here instead of at home, right?"

"Well, when you put it like that, it doesn't seem so bad. It's more the injustice of it all."

Mr. Braverman walked in and dumped his briefcase on his desk. He scanned the room and stopped at me. His eyes lit up. "Austin, it's great to see you. It's not the same when you're not here."

"I'll try to act up more, sir."

"Please do."

Mr. Braverman looked at the rest of the group. "You will all sign in at the end of detention. If you leave before then, you won't get credit. Besides that, I don't care what you do as long as you do it quietly. Wake me if there are any issues." He plopped down in his chair, put his feet up on the desk, and was snoring within six seconds.

I reached into my bag and pulled out a small paper bag. "I brought you something," I whispered to Sophie.

"What?"

"Cookies. For our first detention date."

"Let's hope it's also the last," she said, smiling.

"I'd rather be in detention with you than well, anywhere with anyone else." Suddenly, Mr. Braverman's snoring was super interesting as I realized I had started to blush.

~

THE NEXT DAY at school was another fabulous day. It started off with a before-school meeting. There's nothing that adolescent kids love more than getting up early to receive more schooling and bad principaling.

There were roughly fifty of us in the school auditorium for the kickoff to the National Junior Honors Society push. I didn't really care all that much about it. My mother wanted me to do it. My sister went through it two years ago. All I knew was that it involved a whole bunch of community service, which meant less time to read, build stuff, blow stuff up via science, and play video games.

Sophie, Ben, Just Charles, Randy, and Ditzy Dayna were there, among others. I wasn't sure if Dayna was just in the wrong meeting or what, but I didn't want to make her feel bad.

Dr. Dinkledorf walked across the stage of the auditorium and stopped in front of the podium. He slugged down what seemed like half a gallon of coffee and then began. "Good morning. I know most of you are only here because your parents told you to come, but I want to ensure you that the NJHS, or National Junior Honors Society, is actually quite fun. It is true that you have to perform twenty hours of community service in each of the next three quarters, but I promise you that you will be helping those in need and most of you might even enjoy it."

Ditzy Dayna's hand slowly rose above the crowd.

Dr. Dinkledorf frowned and said, "Dayna, what are you doing here? Umm, what can I help you with?"

"This isn't New Jersey Health Services?"

"No. This isn't even New Jersey." He shook his head and continued, "There will be plenty of different types of activities you can sign up for. There will be blood drives, food drives, and opportunities to volunteer at a retirement home, Vintage Retirement Community."

I knew it well. Our band had performed there over the summer. We rocked those old farts.

Randy said, loud enough for everyone to hear, "Dinkledork is probably trying to get his foot in the door."

A few idiots laughed as they always did when Randy said something. He could walk in the room and say, "Hi," and half the idiots around him would think it was the most-clever thing ever said by a human being.

Thankfully, there wasn't much else to the Honors Society meeting. I planned to put down a whole bunch of stuff I wanted to volunteer for and then suck it up and do it. I wasn't looking forward to it, but whatever.

The official school day started off in Advisory, as always. I sat next to Just Charles, waiting for the Speaker of Doom to crackle and begin the morning announcements.

"What do you think of the new V.P.?" Just Charles asked.

"Umm, she's a psycho."

"She seems kinda nice to me."

"She threw a frog eyeball at me."

"In fairness, you started it."

"True, but I'm pretty certain the average person would've just chucked it in the garbage or an eyeball recycling bin rather than given it back."

"Fair point," Just Charles said.

The Speaker of Doom crackled. Principal Buthaire's voice squeaked, "Yesterday was a banner day at Cherry Avenue Middle School, perhaps across the whole country. Today, we will change the face of education and student achievement. Together, with the lovely and talented Ms. Pierre, who has already endeared herself to so many of you."

"What? It was like six hours. And she's terrible."

"Marcus did say that she farted on him when he was picking up his backpack," Just Charles whispered.

Prince Butt Hair continued, "We will be implementing a revolutionary new student behavior system. Good behavior will be rewarded with the first-ever behavioral currency, Buthaire Bucks!"

"This is terrible," I whispered to Just Charles. On the plus side, we were totally going to call them Butt Bucks.

"Buthaire Bucks will be used to gain access to student events and after-school programs. If you are caught doing something good, you will receive additional Buthaire Bucks. If not, you might owe the school some. Those who embody the spirit of the code of conduct will be handsomely rewarded. Those who don't, won't. An updated version of the code of conduct will be distributed by the end of the day."

"And there you have it. He's going to bribe us to follow his stupid rules. This is bad."

I read through the entire seventy-page code of conduct that was posted online in the student portal. I needed to know every in and out, every inch of fine print that Buthaire could use to smack me down with detentions, or worse, expel me. I'm sure he's already put me on the waiting list at LaSalle Military Academy, the foremost authority on crushing problem children into submission.

There were so many red flags, I can't even list them all. Buthaire Bucks would be given for ratting out peers who broke the rules, getting As on tests, and wearing dull colors, while you would lose Butt Bucks for being late, getting detention, failing tests, going to the bathroom, and something straight-up psycho- for fraternizing with poorly-ranked peers. My friends were going to lose a lot of Butt Bucks for hanging out with me. Of that I was sure.

I walked into the Atrium at school, not sure what to expect. I didn't know if kids would be wearing brown monk robes, diapers, or both, or running away from me every time I got too close to them. The code didn't distinctly say that kids would lose points for hanging out with me specifically, but it was pretty obvious who it was directed at.

But outside of a few kids in black clothing, there was no sign of anything crazy until second period. That's when I realized the new SBS (Student Behavior System), which also could stand for Sweaty Butt Stench because they were synonymous, was going to rapidly change daily life at Cherry Avenue Middle School.

Dr. Dinkledorf stopped abruptly during an important lesson on something not important enough to remember. He looked at Chad Davies, who was wiggling in his chair like an earthquake had just hit the square tile under his desk.

"Do you have to go to the bathroom, Mr. Davies?"

"It's against the code," he said, crossing his legs.

"To go to the bathroom?" Dr. Dinkledorf asked. He looked me. "Is it? Austin?"

"Yes, sir."

"Are Butt Bucks, er Bhutaire Bucks that important that you're gonna pee in your pants?"

"Am not," Chad said.

"Are too," Dr. Dinkledorf responded.

"What can you buy with Buthaire Bucks anyway?" Tara Spiegel asked.

Chase Cartwright said, "Monica Winslow said you could buy a car. Prince Butt Hair made some deal with her dad's car dealership."

"What are you gonna do with a car in seventh grade?" Dr. Dinkledorf asked. "Can teachers earn Buthaire Bucks? I could upgrade my ride. Wait, what am I talking about? I hate everything about this new system."

"I heard you can nap in the teacher's lounge," Audra

Phillips said. "And change teachers if you want to. Who else teaches history, Dr. Dinkledorf?"

Dr. Dinkledorf's face dropped.

Audra added quickly, "Asking for a friend."

~

EVERYONE WAS CONFUSED about the new system. So many ridiculous rumors were going around I couldn't even keep track of them. Butt Bucks could be used for Bitcoin, Caribbean cruises, and even for luxury seating on the school bus. And things got downright wacky that afternoon.

Ben tapped me on the shoulder as I packed up my bag at my locker.

"Dude, you gotta check this out," he said, flustered.

"There's a big hullabaloo in the Atrium."

"What's a hullabaloo?" I asked.

"I don't really know. My grandfather says it all the time."

"Oh, okay. Sounds serious."

"It does. That's why I used it."

I followed Ben as we navigated the packed halls into the Atrium. A crowd had gathered in front of the main wall. Kids were standing and staring at the video screen that we had seen being installed just before the assembly. I nudged my way through the crowd until I could get a good view of the new screen.

They definitely weren't playing video games. On the screen were names of hundreds of students with numbers next to each one. The top of the board was labeled, SBS Rankings.

"He's going to broadcast everyone's score. People are going to be tattling on those above them and afraid to hang out with those below them," I said.

"This is bad," Ben said.

〜

THE NEXT DAY WAS WORSE. It appeared as if Principal Buthaire's great mood had worn off. He was basically chasing me around with a fly swatter all day. I mean that figuratively rather than literally, because that would just be weird.

The Speaker of Doom crackled and echoed, "A special congratulations to our top ten student behavior achievers. They are Ava Sasser, Jennifer Plotkin, Margaret Blatch, Jason Tannen, Devan Moran, Crystal Rivers, Zack Franklin, Erika San Antonio, Scott Washington, and Randolph Warblemacher."

"Ugh," I said. At least they called him Randolph. But then it got even worse.

The Speaker of Doom continued, "At the bottom of list with behavior deemed unbecoming of a Gopher, we are disappointed in Marcus Judd, Jimmy Bambino, Wendy Grier, Amanda Gluskin, Justin Gant, Luke Hill, Benjamin Gordon, Charles Zaino, Sophie Rodriguez, and you guessed it, Austin Davenport."

The day pretty much continued like that. Principal Buthaire stopped me as I was rushing on my way to lunch. Nobody cared if I was late to lunch. I wasn't missing anything, but apparently the world ends if kids are in the hallway after the bell.

The bell rang as I scooted around the corner, only about twenty seconds from the cafeteria doors when Principal Bhuthaire slipped out of the utility closet and stopped in front of me. Surprised and unable to avoid him, I stopped short and looked up at him.

"You're late, Misterrrr Davenport," he said, monotone.

I thought I would try a new tactic. "I'm sorry, sir."

"Your shirt's not tucked in. Your shoes are untied. Those are clear dress code violations."

"I'm sorry, sir."

"No excuses? No snippy remarks?" Prince Butt Hair said, handing me a detention slip.

"No, sir. Do you think we can just start over? This is getting ridiculous. You're jumping out of supply closets to catch me being late."

Principal Buthaire nodded. "If that's what you want."

"Yes, I do."

"Okay. Here goes. You're late, mister Davenport. Your shirt's not tucked in. Your shoes are untied. Here is your detention slip."

I was so angry. "You just gave me one for the same stuff!"

Principal Butt Hair tore off another detention slip and held it out for me. "Disrespectful communication to authority figures."

I grabbed the detention slip and said, "Good day, sir." I wanted to follow with the harsh, but well-deserved Willie Wonka continuation, "I said, good day, sir!", but I felt that would just get me into more trouble. That doesn't always stop me, but I was at my wit's end.

I walked around Principal Buthaire and continued toward the cafeteria. Three detentions? It serves me right for thinking the guy was anything but a psycho.

Sophie, Ben, and Sammie were waiting on the hot lunch line, looking for me. I walked up to them just shaking my head.

"What's the matter?" Sophie asked.

"Everything. Butt Hair was waiting for me in the supply closet to give me a detention for being late. I asked him if we could start over, meaning our whole relationship, and he started the conversation over and gave me a second detention for the same lateness. And then a third for arguing about it."

"That's so unfair," Sammie said.

Sophie looked so angry I thought she was going to run out of the room, grab her archery gear, and let a few shots rip at Prince Butt Hair like she did at the Medieval Renaissance Fair.

"I can't believe he's doing this," Ben said. "I mean, what did I ever do to deserve being at the bottom of the student behavior wall?"

"I think you're missing the point," I said, angrily. "She was talking about how unfair it is to me."

"Guys," Sophie said. "There's no sense in us all arguing. He's made us all look stupid. And Austin has to deal with it like ten times worse than anyone else. Let's talk about something good."

"Like what?" I asked, still a little mad.

Sophie looked at me and said, "Well, I can't wait to go to the Halloween dance with you. Last year at the dance was our first date."

"I feel like a doofus now," I said, smiling. My cheeks reddened a little. "That'll be fun."

"I'm glad you won't have to save the dance this time," Sophie said, laughing.

"That was epic, though, wasn't it?"

"It was," Sophie said, and then to Sammie, "Are you gonna go with anyone?"

"I'll probably just go with Ben."

I looked at Ben. He was more surprised than anyone.

Sammie continued, "I'm done with boys after Derek and Randy."

"I'm a boy!" Ben said.

"I didn't mean like that. You're like my brother."

I shrugged and said, "Maybe you should just be done with idiots and not boys?"

Sammie nearly snarled at me, but I think she understood my point.

≈

THE NEXT DAY we hopped off the bus and headed into the Atrium. Most of the kids there were searching for their names and scores up on the SBS board, or what had quickly become known as "Heroes" and "Zeroes", and I, Austin Davenport, was Captain Zero.

Or maybe it should've been Captain Negative. I apparently owed Principal Butt Hair Butt Bucks after my detention trifecta on the way to lunch. My friends and I were at the bottom of the student behavior board in the Atrium again.

"Nice work, Austin," Scottie Washington said with a smile. "You blew us Zeroes all away. You must've had to try pretty hard to go negative."

I shrugged. "It's pretty easy when Butt Hair hates you. He literally jumped out of a supply closet to catch me being late for lunch."

"Whoa, he really hates you. Keep up the good work!" Scottie yelled as he ran to class.

"Thanks," I called after him. "I guess."

On my way to Advisory, Luke caught up to me and Just Charles. Luke's class was only a few doors past ours.

"You're never gonna believe this," Luke said.

"We never do," I responded.

"Very funny. I asked Jasmine Jane to the dance and she said yes!"

"Sweet. Cheryl and I are going, too," Just Charles said.

"Now, we just gotta get Gordo a date," Luke said.

"He might go with Sammie," I said.

Luke shrugged as we arrived outside our Advisory room. "Later, fellas!"

"Adiós, muchacho," I said.

The Speaker of Doom crackled as we slipped into our seats. "Blah, blah, blah, blah, blah, and blah."

My friends and I took the same bashing as the day before. I didn't really care. I was used to it. I felt bad for my crew. They didn't deserve to get ridiculed just for being friends with me. True, Sophie did get detention, but that wasn't fair, either. It was revenge for sticking it to Prince, actually Emperor Butt Hair, during the Medieval quest we went on at the Renaissance fair.

The Speaker of Doom finally said something that was at least somewhat important. "The volunteer schedules for the National Junior Honors Society have been completed by Dr. Dinkledorf. Please see him during the course of the week to pick up your copy if you are participating. Sessions start as early as this weekend."

∾

AFTER SCHOOL WAS OVER, I headed to the bus with Ben. Everyone in the Atrium was still going crazy over the Heroes and Zeroes board, constantly checking to see where they ranked and who they were ahead of. I knew where I stood. Dead last. Captain Negative.

"If this wasn't so unfair, do you think I'd care about being last?" I asked Ben.

"Maybe, but probably not. Can I ask you a serious question?"

"Sure," I said, not sure about what was so serious.

"How does someone owe Buthaire Butt Bucks?" Ben asked, trying not to laugh.

"I don't know. I don't even recognize it as a legitimate currency."

"I just can't believe everyone is going so crazy about this."

"This is bad." Those three words basically summed up my entire middle school existence.

4

I made my way to the bus. I was looking forward to a quiet bus ride home. Sammie had cheerleading practice and Derek had football practice, which meant Ben and I could just chill without gossip or spit balls in our ears. Of course, Prince Butt Hair had to go and ruin that.

Principal Buthaire was waiting for me as I exited the building, Ms. Pierre at his side. I slipped behind Ben and tried to hide on the far side of him, but Prince Butt Hair cut through the foot traffic, nearly knocking over some sixth grader on crutches, and stood in front of me. I had no place to hide. Ben's backpack was nowhere near big enough and that was my only option.

He looked at Ms. Pierre and whispered with a smile, "Watch how it's done, Anne." Prince Butt Hair turned to me and said, "Good afternoon, Misterrrr Davenport. Mr. Gordon."

"Hello, Principal Buthaire," I said, monotone. I looked at Ms. Pierre and said, "Good afternoon, Mizzzz Pierre," trying to make sure I said it correctly. "I'm late for my bus," I said, trying to step around my butt-brained principal.

Principal Buthaire stepped in front of me, blocking my path again. "Your bus driver will wait," he said, laughing.

I didn't know if he was laughing because he knew there was no way in the world my bus driver would wait or if there was something else. Typically, if he was laughing, it was at me or what he was about to do to me.

"What's so funny, sir?"

"I noticed your score under the new system. It was disappointing, but expected."

I was so tired of him, I just didn't care anymore. "My mother always says you tend to get what you expect."

"So, you're saying this is my fault? Take responsibility for your actions, mister, and maybe you wouldn't be in detention all the time. I don't understand you. You get good grades, yet you can't seem to grasp the fact that if you stay in line and conform, you would be much better off."

I looked past Principal Buthaire and Ms. Pierre as my bus pulled away. "There goes my bus," I said, frustrated. I looked back at Prince Butt Face and said, "You've treated me like a problem kid from day one, before you even knew me."

"I believe that was a discussion we had after I caught you roaming the halls after the bell, a clear rule violation?"

Principal Buthaire nodded and smiled at Ms. Pierre, as if he had just landed the decisive blow in the greatest battle of all time. She smiled back.

"Yep, you're right. I was late on the first day in a new school like half the kids in the world and I've been paying for it ever since. Well, this has been fun, but Benjamin and I have to go milk his cat."

"Dude, that's weird," Ben said, unhelpfully.

"This has been a productive talk," Principal Buthaire said.

I wasn't sure what conversation he was talking about. Ours certainly wasn't productive.

He continued, "Oh, I wanted to tell you. We have a special announcement tomorrow that I'm sure you'll particularly like."

Ahh, farts.

～

SOMEHOW, I sank lower in the rankings on the Zeroes board and I was already dead last. Apparently, I was close to getting my locker foreclosed on. Some kids were speculating that I would have to file for bankruptcy. I was already emotionally bankrupt. I sat in Advisory, my head on my desk. Feedback echoed from the Speaker of Doom to start the morning announcements, but I didn't even budge.

Principal Buthaire was delivering the morning announcements, which only meant he was about to administer more pain. "Good morning, Gophers. Tickets are now available for the Halloween Dance. We've got some serious fun planned."

I sprung up in my seat and looked at Just Charles. "What is going on?"

"I think we're in Superman's Bizarro world. Or Principal Buthaire had some sort of Freaky Friday curse. Maybe he switched bodies with someone...nice."

Prince Butt Head continued, "We're going to have a live band, Goat Turd! That sounds gross, but I'm sure everyone will love them."

My Advisory class was going nuts. Everybody loved Goat Turd. They were an awesome band and pretty cool dudes. I had met them over the summer at the Battle of the Bands contest we entered. I couldn't believe what was going on.

"What's the catch?" Mrs. Callahan asked. Even she knew it was getting bizarre.

And then the Speaker of Doom delivered the catch. "Those who wish to participate must have one hundred Buthaire Bucks."

Half my class groaned. Joey Kim yelled out, "A hundred Butt Bucks! Half the school won't be able to go."

I put my head back down on my desk. "That's the point," I said to no one in particular.

Just Charles said, "Do you think they even considered Mayhem Mad Men?"

"Yeah, right," I said, with a sarcastic chuckle.

∾

A TEAM MEETING WAS CALLED. Of course, we met at Frank's Pizza, headquarters of our growing group of angry activists. Sophie, Ben, Sammie, Luke, Just Charles, and Cheryl Van Snoogle-Something were there along with a few chewed-up pizza crusts.

Ben called the meeting to order as he always did by banging the parmesan cheese dispenser on the table. "This begins our meeting. We welcome our newest member, Cheryl Van Snoogle-Something. So very excited to have you on the team. Your connections at the Gopher Gazette, our school newspaper, will be a nice addition to our team."

"Happy to be here. I actually started writing an article about how unfair the new student behavior system is for the next edition of the Gopher Gazette."

"I hate being a Gopher, but I'm a big fan of the name, Gopher Gazette. Is that weird?" I asked.

"Not at all," Ben said.

"That's great news, by the way," I said to Cheryl. I looked

at the rest of the crew. "We find ourselves in familiar territory, fighting against a corrupt, oppressive system. I don't know about you, but I've had enough."

"What do we do?" Sophie asked.

"We do the opposite of what we did last year. We take down the dance," Ben said.

"That was you?" Cheryl asked. "That was awesome. I heard it was you guys, but nobody knew for sure."

"It's a long story, but Ben and I built the foam machine. That's still top-secret information. I'm sure Butt Hair would still give me like a thousand detentions if he found out it was me."

"My lips are sealed."

"How would we take down the dance?" Luke asked.

"I think we should take down the whole system," I said.

"But how?" Just Charles asked.

"We be the best Zeroes we can be. We break every rule, thwart Butt Hair at every turn."

"And we take down the dance," Ben said.

Luke asked, "Do we have to? I have a date. Jasmine Jane…"

"You don't have enough Butt Bucks to go, so Jasmine Jane is gonna go with someone else," Sammie said.

Luke pounded the table. "The dance is goin' down!"

"But how?" Just Charles asked again. "He can't just exclude us, can he?"

"When he canceled the dance last year, the Board of Education put it back on. Why don't we get the Board to force him to let us go?" Sophie asked.

"I can write an article about that, too. Maybe even interview some board members," Cheryl Van Snoogle-Something said.

"I think that's our best shot right now," I said. "Everyone

agree?"

The whole team nodded in unison.

"If the board doesn't help us, then we wreak Zero mayhem," Ben said.

"We wreak a lot of mayhem," I said.

"I meant with a capital Z, Zero."

"Oh, right."

"We need a secret team name," Luke said, excitedly.

"Oh, God." I immediately thought of the time we named our band. Luke thought that Lit Fart was a good option.

"We're the Freedom Fighters, end of story," I said.

"That's not very freedom-like, but I like it," Sophie said.

"I'm sorry, but we went down this path with the band and it was not a good one."

"Okay, Freedom Fighters," Ben said, "We need to prepare a plan for the Board to get us into the dance and let's start brain storming on how we can wreak havoc on the new student behavior system."

"It's time to shave some Butt Hair," Luke said, smiling. "Who's with me?"

The girls all rolled their eyes.

I just shook my head and said, "Are you sure Jasmine Jane said yes?"

"Yeah, can I bring her next time? Everyone has a girl-friend here, but me. Well, except Ben, but that's to be expected."

"Hey!" Ben said, annoyed.

"This isn't date night. We're fighting evil here," I said, again shaking my head. My friends, particularly Luke, caused me to do that quite often.

The next few days were going to be interesting. We were going to begin dismantling the system. And little did we know, my nemesis had a few surprises in store for us, too.

5

I was pretty excited to go to school the next day. I knew Principal Buthaire would find some way to give me detention for having skin or something. He'd be like, "Misterrrr Davenport, your epidermis is showing! Dee-tent-shawn!" And there would be nothing I could do. Actually, what he did the next day was much worse.

The Speaker of Doom crackled and broadcasted a soul-crushing message from Ms. Pierre. "Good morning, Gophers! I am happy to announce enhancements to our Student Behavior System! It was wonderful getting to know most of you yesterday. With Principal Buthaire's assistance, we identified key leaders within the school that we have chosen to act as Peer Review Counselors to help us with our new system."

Just Charles and I looked at each other, both of us holding in puke. I heard a lot of hwullahing through the hallways from other classrooms, too.

Ms. Pierre named a whole bunch of sixth graders that I didn't know and then moved onto my grade. "Jayden Johnson, Nick DeRozan, Derek Davenport..."

"Ahh, farts!" I yelled. The entire class looked at me. "Sorry, Mrs. Callahan."

"No, I think you hit the nail on the head with that one."

Ms. Pierre finished up, "Brody Cook and Peyton Pruitt. That's it for the Peer Review Committee in seventh grade." She went on to announce the eighth graders.

Nearly the entire class groaned.

"Did she say Randy?" I asked the class.

"I don't think so," Just Charles said.

"Oh, my God. I can't believe it." I was shocked. Randy wasn't a Peer Review Counselor. He must've still been on Prince Butt Hair's naughty list after the whole website incident. Maybe you remember that one from the science fair story.

And then I thought I might throw up in my mouth.

Ms. Pierre said, "Peer Review Counselor team leaders are Randy Warblemacher, Regan Storm, Zachary Young, and Helena Avery."

There were definite signs of hwullahing from the hallway. I felt bad for Zorch, my friend and custodian at Cherry Avenue. I was pretty certain he'd be mopping up a lot of vomit after this Speaker of Doom doozy.

After Advisory was over, I met up with Just Charles and Cheryl Van Snoogle-Something in the Atrium.

Cheryl handed me a piece of paper and said, "Read this and keep it quiet." She glanced around nervously.

I scanned the paper quickly. It was the article she was submitting to the Gopher Gazette. It was awesome. "Socialistic dystopian oppression? I mean I agree with you, but none of these boneheads are gonna know what any of that means." I actually didn't either, but I didn't want to look stupid.

Cheryl looked disappointed.

"Otherwise, it's fabulous." I continued reading, "The new Student Behavior System is yet another societal class system that pits one group against another that is bound to reduce educational enrichment and destroy what little joy is left in middle school."

"That's legit," Just Charles said.

Before I had a chance to read anymore, a gust of wind cut through the Atrium. The article flew out of my hand. Cheryl ran off to grab it.

I looked over at the double doors that appeared to have opened without assistance and led into the Atrium. Randy and Regan walked in side by side. It wouldn't have surprised me if Randy had abused the handicap button, but those doors didn't even have one. They strutted through the crowd like they were rock stars or royalty or something. Regan's blonde hair flew back like she was on a photo shoot. I looked around for giant fans, but couldn't find them anywhere. Randy's hair, of course, didn't budge. His hair, once again, defied the laws of physics and I didn't know how.

"I guess they're back together," I said to Just Charles.

"They're perfect for each other."

I wasn't happy. Randy being back with Regan meant he was going to be extra obnoxious in music, gym, and science. I was surprised his head even fit through the door. This was bad.

~

AND IT GOT BADDER. Gym class was life-ruining, although based on Mr. Muscalini's enthusiasm, you never would've known it. I guess that was because it was my life that was ruined and not his.

As our class stood at the edge of the wrestling mats, Mr. Muscalini yelled, "It's wrestling month! My favorite time of year. We're gonna start things off with a cage match to the death."

Huh? Everyone looked around at each other. Nerd knees were knocking like crazy.

Mr. Muscalini laughed. "Just kidding. But it will be fun. Our two best athletes are going to go head to head to show you what a real wrestling match looks like." He looked down at his clipboard. "Warblemacher?"

Randy stepped forward with a smirk.

"Davenport?"

I knew he wasn't talking about me, but my brother wasn't in our class.

"Where are you, Davenport?"

Everybody stared at me. I stepped forward. "Sir, I think you mixed me up with my brother, Derek."

Mr. Muscalini looked at me and then down at the clipboard. "Oh, I think you're right. Why don't you come on out here anyway? It'll be fun. Warblemacher is a good kid. He'll take it easy on you."

I looked at Randy. He was salivating like he hadn't been fed in weeks and I was a hundred pounds of bacon. And even though Randy was an idiot, even idiots love bacon.

"Sir, he outweighs me by like fifty pounds."

"I'll go easy on him, coach," Randy said, smiling at me.

"Don't let him get inside," Ben said.

"Inside what?" I asked.

"Your circle," Ben said. "Remember your training. Let it be your guide." He was talking about my sword training that he and my father had given me in preparing for the medieval quest I competed in at the Medieval Renaissance Fair.

I nodded to Ben and stepped toward Randy. "You think I don't know how to fight dirty? My brother has been kicking my butt for the past eleven years. And I'm not afraid to bite. These braces are a deadly weapon."

"You're just making this worse for yourself, Davenfart."

My fear made me make it worser. "If I get your jugular, it's not my fault." I wasn't even sure what his jugular was, but I knew it was important.

"I'm gonna break every bone in your body."

As Randy and I faced off in the center of the mat, I decided to take one last shot at getting out of it before I died. "Sir, I think this is a bad idea."

Mr. Muscalini looked up from admiring his alternating peck flexing. "What? Oh yeah, I'm starting to think that, too. But you have to learn from your mistakes, Davenport."

"This was your mistake!"

"You're never gonna learn, Davenport, if you blame everyone but yourself. Now, wrestle!"

Randy surged forward like a rocket, heading straight into my circle. He wrapped his arms around my knees, squeezed and lifted. The force of his attack knocked me back.

"Oh, devastating takedown by Warblemacher!" Mr. Muscalini yelled.

All the athletes cheered, while my nerd buds groaned.

I fell to my butt, and then rolled to my side to avoid a quick pin. In hindsight, I should've just lost on purpose because I was pretty sure I was going to lose not on purpose, too. Randy maneuvered his arms under and around mine, twisting and turning. With my back to Mr. Muscalini, Randy thrust his fist into my ribs. I rolled onto my stomach with a grunt. Randy wrapped me in a full nelson and forced my face into the mat.

Mr. Muscalini yelled, "Davenport is making out with the mat like he's practicing for the prom!"

I had two moves in my bag of tricks. I could bite him, which just thinking about made me sick. Or I could fart, hoping that it would distract him and I could escape. It didn't work often with Derek, but Randy would definitely be grossed out. I struggled to escape as I thought about my next move. I decided to go with the option number two, a full-frontal fart free-for-all.

"Davenport is flopping like a fish out of water!"

I PUSHED out with all my might and let 'er rip. I was hoping for a powerful and noisy fart that would leave no doubt what had happened and hopefully lead to Randy ending the match in a draw, but I got a silent stinker.

I struggled to my knees, waiting for my attack to reach Randy's vulnerable nostrils. He dropped his weight on my back and I fell to my stomach again.

"Are we in the gym or the International House of Pancakes?"

Randy was so quick, I thought he might've transformed into a spider. Before I knew it, he was sitting on my lower back with his hands clasped underneath my chin and pulling up.

Mr. Muscalini bellowed, "The Camel Clutch! Warblemacher! W.W.E. moves are not sanctioned in USA wrestling! But if you're gonna do it, you gotta pull up harder on his chin. He looks more like a seal than a camel."

I was pretty certain I was barking like a seal and spitting like a camel, so he was still doing a pretty good job. I felt my back stretching to its limits. My eyes lost focus.

Mr. Muscalini continued his play by play. "Oh, Davenport's face is reddening. He's getting mad! No, no. I think he's not getting enough air. This is gonna be a crazy finish, folks!"

Mr. Muscalini counted me out, pounding on the mat,

one, two, three. Randy kept crushing me. Ben rushed Randy and knocked him off of me.

I gasped for breath as my body remained stuck in the shape of the letter U.

Randy stood up and stared at Ben. "I like the fight, Gordo, but you should think before you pick one with me."

I lay there, staring at the ceiling, the lights swirling around like strobe lights. Randy stood above me and laughed.

"Okay, somebody carry Davenport off to the side. Let's break up into weight classes."

After all my senses returned and my blood flow increased to the point where I could actually move my limbs, I got matched up with Jesse Tran. I had no interest in wrestling anymore.

I looked at Jesse, pain throbbing in too many places to count. "Dude, how about I let you win? You can just lay on me," I said.

"Dude, that's weird."

I went through the motions for a few minutes, but I eventually ran out of steam. I leaned over with my hands on my knees, breathing deeply. "Yo, dude. I need a break from this. You got any ketchup packets? I used my last one to get out of volleyball last week."

"Yep." He turned his back to Mr. Muscalini and took a necklace out from inside his shirt. It wasn't really a necklace, but one of those protective cases parents use to keep their money dry when going to the beach. He popped it open, slipped out a ketchup packet, and said, "This is my last one. You need to get some refills."

"Absolutely. I'll grab two fistfuls at my next fast food stop."

Jesse handed me the packet. I checked to make sure Mr.

Muscalini wasn't looking in our direction. Surprisingly, he was making his quads dance. I tore open the packet and spread the ketchup on my hands and under my nose. I put my head back and pinched my nose.

"Dude, are you all right?" Jesse asked.

Mr. Muscalini looked over as Jesse escorted me off to the side. "If there's no blood, get up and get it done!"

"We got blood here, sir," Jesse called over to Mr. Muscalini.

"Okay. Bring him to the nurse, I guess."

I was really grateful for Mr. Muscalini's concern. I looked back at Ben who was stuck in a figure-four leg lock by Chase Martin. He waved, as I hustled out of the gym.

The rest of the day was similar to gym class. It was basically one giant Camel Clutch.

∽

DR. DINKLEDORF HANDED out our volunteer schedules in history class. As soon as he handed it to me, three things jumped off the page at me: Me, Randy, and old people. It was not going to be a good combination.

Randy seemed to feel the same way. "Ugh, I got stuck with Davenfart. The only things that smell worse than him are old people. And I got stuck with them, too."

Of course, Regan and a few other idiots laughed.

I was tired of his nonsense. "You think I want to hang out with you, ya putz?"

"Davenfart, I'm gonna crush you in volunteer hours. You're not even gonna know what hit you."

"I actually don't even care if you have more hours than I do as long as I get my twenty."

"Oh, you're gonna get your twenty," he said, laughing.

I had no idea what he was talking about. I was thankful when Dr. Dinkledorf started the lesson. Unfortunately, it was on Neanderthals and how they grunted to communicate. It was only slightly less boring than Randy's charades.

"Is he serious?" I whispered to Ben.

"This is brutal. The retirement home with Randy?"

"Diapers and dorks? This is gonna be horrible."

"Randy wears diapers? I thought you were the only one who did that."

"Funny, Benny boy."

6

I woke up on Saturday morning with a slap on my alarm clock. I didn't mind getting up in the morning because I always pretended my alarm was Derek's face. I always had a positive start to the day. You should try it with your evil sibling sometime.

But then I remembered that it was my first day of volunteering at Vintage Retirement Community: four hours of Bingo! and dentures. It was going to be a riveting day. And my bestie, Randy, would be there. At least Ben and Sophie would be, too.

There were six of us there. Ethan Parks and Bella Romo were the other two. We were split into groups of guys and girls to start, all of us hanging out in the recreation center. The guys played checkers while the girls crocheted old people underwear or something.

I sat across from Malcolm Jabberwocky, a wrinkly dude with thick glasses and perfectly-slicked-back silver hair. He wasn't a very good checkers player, but somehow, he seemed to keep beating me.

"Still got it in my old age!" Malcolm said, as he moved a checker piece toward my back row. "King me, Alvin!"

"It's Austin," I said, annoyed.

"What's that?"

'What's what?'

"What did you say?"

"The first time or the second time?"

"No, I don't like limes."

I kinged Malcolm's piece and looked over at Ben. He was playing checkers with some dude, Carl, who seemingly only shaved half his face that day. Randy played against a sweet granny named Rochelle, while Ethan faced off against a tough-looking woman, Ethel. She had her sleeves rolled up, revealing forearms full of skull tattoos.

"Ha ha! Beat you again, Rochelle!" Randy yelled, laughing, as he double jumped poor old Rochelle's last two pieces.

I whispered to Ben, "Typical."

Ben leaned over to me and said, "Yeah, this isn't any

different than school It almost smells as bad here as it does at Cherry Avenue."

"Yeah, it's not B.O., though. It's more like O.O. Old odor."

"You gonna move, sonny boy?" Malcolm asked, annoyed.

"Oh, sorry." I slid a piece forward, setting up a killer move.

Malcolm reached forward, his robe scraping the table and moving half the pieces on the board. He moved his piece and sat back down. My awesome move had disappeared because the board was now a jumbled mess.

"I gotcha right where I want ya, sonny boy. Hey, who moved these pieces? Fred! We got another cheater!"

"Who's Fred?" I asked.

"I'm not dead yet, Alvin. Still 89 years young."

"Who you kidding, Malcolm? You're older than dirt," Carl said, laughing.

"I like this shirt, Ram Butt," Malcolm said to Carl.

"My name's Ramsbottom, you imbecile!"

"This guy is like Randy at ninety years old," I said to Ben.

"You got candy?" Malcolm yelled.

"No," I said.

"What? I used to date a girl named Candy."

We looked over at Randy. He was playing against Ethel now. They were locked in a staring match, possibly to the death. No pieces had even been moved. I looked over at Sophie and Bella. They were smiling and laughing with a bunch of old ladies and one man, having a ton of fun crocheting. Who knew it could be so exciting?

"Alvin! You're up, Butter Cup."

Ugh. I made my move and studied Malcolm as he scanned the board.

He leaned over the board and reached out to move a

piece on my half of the board. My mouth dropped open as his other hand slid underneath his chest and grabbed one of my pieces off the board.

"He's cheating," I said to Ben. "He's blatantly taking my pieces off the board!"

"Just let him win, dude," Ben said.

"I can't wait until this is over. I want to crochet some underwear. They look cozy."

"Is it almost twelve?" Carl asked.

"Yes, is that lunch time?" Ben asked.

"No, I got a farting contest set up with Charlie over there, the crocheting moron. He's trying to get Edna to go out with him. She accidentally witnessed our farting contest once, so I doubt she'll say yes. But he's better than Jabberwocky over here."

"It doesn't smell like cocky," Malcolm said. He looked at me. "You want to check my diaper to make sure?"

"Umm, no."

"He's a volunteer, Malcolm. Not a saint!" Carl said, laughing.

"What day is it?" Malcolm asked.

"Saturday," I said, grumpily. It reminded me that it was Saturday and I was playing checkers with a cheating elderly Randy.

"Visiting day," Malcolm said. "My grandson should be here soon."

"He's not coming," Carl said. "He never does."

The crocheting crew walked over our way.

Sophie smiled at me, while pushing a woman in a wheelchair. "How's it going?"

"Great," I said, sarcastically.

"We're going to get Rose some fresh air. You guys want to come?"

"Carl and Charlie have a farting contest, so after that, we'll need some fresh air. Sounds good."

"You ready, Ramsbottom?" Charlie asked, as he caned his way toward us.

Before waiting for an answer, Charlie let out a massive fart that may have actually shaken the floor.

"Gross!" Randy said, jumping out of his chair.

Charlie stopped mid-walk, seemingly frozen.

"Charlie, are you okay?" Bella asked, stopping beside him.

"Oops," he said. "I think I lost."

"Lost what?" Bella asked.

"The contest."

"But Carl hasn't even gone-" I said, and then, "Oh."

"I think we should get some fresh air now," Ben said.

Charlie slapped Randy on the shoulder. "Randolph, do me a solid, will ya and you know, take a quick peek back there and see if I made a solid? It might be hard to tell because I peed in my diaper twice already. Or was it three times?"

The look on Randy's face made it all worth it. I'm pretty certain he threw up in his mouth. I wasn't happy at all being there with Malcolm. He was a crotchety old cheater who called me by the wrong name. Sound familiar? I didn't want to go back. It was like hanging out with Randy. And Randy. What could be worse than that? Not much. Maybe adding Prince Butt Hair to that party would be worse, but that's about it.

∼

ON MONDAY MORNING, Ben, Sammie, and I met up with Sophie, Just Charles, and Cheryl in the Atrium before school started. I looked at the Student Behavior System score board and actually smiled. I couldn't wait to take that stupid system down.

Cheryl leaned in and whispered to us, "My article is coming out this morning. It should've gone to the printer this weekend."

Jake Levine walked by, staring at Cheryl or Just Charles.

"What's with him?" I asked.

"I don't know," Sophie said. "But a lot of people are staring at us. Well, Cheryl."

"Nobody ever stares at me," Cheryl said.

"Just Charles did in Spanish class all of sixth grade," Sammie said.

"Did not," Just Charles said. "But seriously, this is weird."

Amanda Gluskin walked by, holding a blue piece of paper. Her eyes were locked on Cheryl and looked like they might shoot fire. She crumpled up the paper and tossed it at Cheryl's feet.

"What is going on?" Cheryl said, her voice shaking.

"I don't know, but she had that look in her eye when she put me in the Camel Clutch last year in the science fair."

"It's not a good sign," Ben said, picking up the crumpled paper.

"Today was supposed to be a great day with the new article. I thought most of the kids would be happy," Cheryl said, her brow furrowed.

Ben opened up the paper and said, "It's the Gazette. The front page reads, Buthaire Bucks A Hit by Cheryl Van Snoogle-Something."

"What? That's not what I wrote," Cheryl said, angrily.

Ben continued, "The dynamic duo of Principal Buthaire and Vice Principal Pierre have a hit on their hands. No, they haven't been working with Mrs. Funderbunk on a theatrical masterpiece. It's Buthaire Bucks. Better than Bitcoin, Buthaire Bucks are a new currency in behavior." Ben looked up at the rest of us. "Should I continue?"

"No," Cheryl said, angrily. She snatched the paper out of Ben's hand and held it up over her head. She yelled out, "I did not write this piece of garbage! My article was the exact opposite of this! Somebody please tell Amanda Gluskin that before I end up in the Camel Clutch!"

It wasn't often that school went wrong so early in the day, like before the first bell rang for Advisory. And it got worse. The Peer Review Committee was cracking down like crazy. As Just Charles and I headed to Advisory, Randy was waiting for me in the doorway, his annoying face looking unimpressed, as he scanned me up and down.

"What are you doing here?" I asked. "It's bad enough I have to see you over the weekends. Now, you're waiting for me in class?"

"I'm not here to socialize, Davenfart. I have a job to do. And unfortunately, with your behavior, I'm gonna have a lot of work to do."

"Get out of the doorway, idiot," I said. "I don't have time for your nonsense." I tried to walk past him, but he blocked me.

I turned around to find Nick DeRozan standing behind us. I took a deep breath and exhaled. I turned back to Randy.

"This is ridiculous," Just Charles said.

"Is your unsanctioned backpack nonsense? It's over-sized. How about your hair? It's too long on the sides."

"So is yours," I said.

"This isn't about me, Davenfart. This is about your constant flouting of the rules."

"Yes, I'm a flouter," I said sarcastically. "Or is it a floutist?"

Randy scratched his porcelain face. "I'll have to get back you on that, but my complaints stand, Davenfart. Get a haircut or we'll shave your head."

"You can't do that, idiot."

"Try me."

"No, I don't want to. I've tried. I don't like you. It's not something I want to try again."

It was the weirdest interaction I'd ever had with a bully or perhaps anyone.

Randy nodded to Nick. "Bring your buzzer in tomorrow. I'll let you do it."

"I don't have one," Nick's deep voice bellowed.

"Then buy one," Randy said, annoyed.

"That's like three weeks of my allowance."

If I hadn't been in a pretty big pickle, it would've been funny seeing someone as manly as Nick talking about his allowance.

Randy shrugged. "We'll expense it."

"Okay, boss," Nick said.

"You have an expense account?" I asked, horrified.

Randy just smirked. "I mean it, Davenfart. Clean up that mop. Or I'll use your head to mop the wrestling mat again, because that was fun."

∼

I WAS SO angry in Advisory that I decided to head to Max's for a quick bathroom break. It was a long walk to the east wing, but a regular bathroom break wasn't gonna cut it. If you haven't heard me talk of Max before, let's just say he was the biggest mystery of middle school. Well, besides why Sophie was my girlfriend. Max ran a private bathroom in the public school. He charged U.S. Dollars for usage. I hoped he hadn't been forced to switch to Butt Bucks.

Cutting edge and constantly changing, Max's Comfort Station was a bathroom oasis. In the past, there were pool tables, massage tables, dining room tables. A serious number of tables. There were hot tubs, massage chairs, video games, and gourmet foods.

As I pushed the door open to Max's, a surge of energy rushed through me. I hadn't felt that good in a while. Still, after my run-in with Randy, I needed meditation, gourmet chocolate, or essential oils. I also figured there was a strong possibility that Max had rejiggered his comfort station to include a barber or even a high-end salon, so I could get Randy off my back.

I walked in, expecting high fives, and to be wowed. Well, I was wowed. But not in a good way. Normally, I got a warm greeting. He called me Aus the Boss, usually. But Max was asleep like he had passed out from boredom. His snore echoed through the tiled bathroom. There were no hot tubs or video games, and the cheese looked funky.

The door slammed shut behind me. Max jolted awake. "What the-"

"Max? Are you okay?" I asked, stepping forward slowly.

"Aus, dude," was all he said, shaking his head.

I looked around at the dank bathroom surrounding us. "What, what happened to this place?" I asked.

Max stood up and attempted to pat down his wavy hair. "Welcome to the barren wasteland that is Max's Uncomfortable Station."

"What are you talking about? I don't understand."

"Revenue has cratered. Nobody goes to the bathroom anymore. I mean, don't they have to? It's like the dirty water debacle at the Medieval Renaissance Fair all over again."

"What do you mean, people aren't going to the bathroom anymore? This place was killing it last time I was here."

Max shrugged. "Subscriptions are being canceled left and right. The new Student Behavior System or whatever."

"Oh, no. They lose Butt Bucks if they go to the bathroom. I didn't even think of that."

"I'd offer you a drink, but I didn't even bother restocking. At first, I thought it would be okay, but things fell off a cliff once this Peer Review Committee started up."

"I'm still in shock."

"I'm gonna have to go back to school," Max said, shaking his head.

I didn't know what to say. I didn't know how old he was or where he had come from. "Where would you go?"

"Well, technically I'm still in eighth grade, I guess. I haven't been to class in fourteen years though, so I'm not sure how that would work." He changed the subject. "Are they wearing diapers?"

"I don't know. I hadn't even thought about not going to the bathroom to save Butt Bucks. Between you and me, I'm gonna take the whole system down."

Max smiled for the first time. "I knew you would have a plan, bro."

My mind lit up like a lightbulb. Diapers. "Dude, what do you say about a 50/50 joint venture, selling diapers out of a vending machine?"

"I think you're onto something, Davenport. I'll look into it. I feel like I have a purpose again."

∽

THE BEST PART of the day and really only good part of the day was lunch. It wasn't because of the lunch, because if you've been paying even a little bit of attention, you know that we put our lives on the line every time we hit the hot-food line.

I sat with Ben, Sophie, and Just Charles, checking my

food for bandaids and any other potential foreign matter. Sometimes the food needed a little extra crunch, but I drew the lines at band aids.

"Can you believe what Butt Hair did to Cheryl?" Sophie asked. "It's just not fair."

"I can believe it. It's Butt Hair we're talking about."

"Her message needs to get out there," Just Charles said.

"It still can. Who says the Gopher Gazette is the only newspaper to publish her article?"

"What are you thinking?" Ben said.

"We can just publish it online or Instagram or send it around on Snap Chat," I said.

"We can get Calvin from Channel 2 News," Sophie added.

"If we're the Freedom Fighters, we should start the Freedom Forum, where we can spread news, share ideas," I said.

"She's gonna love this," Just Charles said.

"And Butt Hair is gonna hate it," I said, a smile spreading across my face.

7

That night, we had a lot of work to do. I left the Freedom Forum to the rest of the crew, while I planned out how we were going to take down the dance. After dinner, I sat down with my mother in the den.

"Hey, Mom? I've got a question for you."

She closed her laptop and placed it onto the couch next to her. "What is it, sweetie?"

"Can the school keep certain kids from going to the dance?"

"What do you mean?"

"Well, Butt Hair, er Principal Buthaire started this stupid new system that basically scores and ranks kids based on how well they follow the horrible code of conduct."

"Okay, I'm following you," my mother said. "So, if you don't follow the rules, you don't score well, and then you can't go to the dance?"

"You're pretty smart," I said.

"Where do you think you get it from?" she asked, laughing.

"I wonder what happened to Derek," I said, smirking.

"Funny. Well, I think that the school does have the right to keep students who are deemed behavioral problems or don't make the grades from going."

"What if the way behavioral problems are determined is unfair?"

"This whole new system Butt Hair implemented?"

"Mom!"

"Sorry, honey. Butt Hair the perfect nickname for him. I'm just upset you beat me to it."

"It is pretty good. So, what if the system is bad?"

"Then take it down," she said, simply.

"I think I'm going to have to give another speech."

❦

THE NEXT DAY was pretty crazy. The Freedom Forum was the talk of the school. And I think Randy knew I was behind it. I never said he was dumb. He's just an idiot. There's a difference. He walked up to me in the Atrium, shaking his head.

"I see you didn't get your hair cut. I guess you were busy with other things." Randy's annoying voice said from his annoying face.

"I see you didn't get yours cut, either."

"I make the rules, so it doesn't matter."

"I flout the rules. I'm a floutist."

"You're a foolish flouterer, is what you are."

"Enjoy this while it lasts. Your time is running out," I said as firmly as I could.

"What are you gonna do about it, Davenfart?"

"Don't you worry about it, Randolph. I'm gonna take you down. Take you down to Chinatown."

"Ooh, I love Chinatown. Did you ever eat at Dah How? It's my favorite restaurant."

"No, I love Chinatown, too. I'll try it. Thanks for the tip, idiot."

"No problem, jerk wad." Randy points to his own eyes and then to me. "I'm watching you, Davenfart. You so much as let out even a little bit of a squeaker of a fart and I'm gonna know about it."

"Dude, that's weird."

"That's the world we live in."

"Is it, though?"

"I'm more certain about that than anything I've ever been certain of in my life," Randy said. "Except hating the sight of you."

"We have something in common. I hate your face, too. I'll let you know how the restaurant goes." I turned and walked away.

"Try the sesame chicken. It's so good, dork face."

~

OF COURSE, everyone thought I was responsible for the Freedom Forum. I didn't tell anyone one way or the other, but it felt nice to get credit for something good than blamed for something I didn't do, which was basically every interaction I had with Principal Buthaire.

Jay Parnell and Kieran Murphy walked up to Sophie and me after lunch.

"Nice work, bro," Jay said with a thumbs up.

"I don't know what you're talking about, dude," I said, as I kept walking.

I did a double take as one of the security cameras caught my eye.

"Did you see that?"

"See what?" Sophie asked.

"The camera. I think it zoomed in."

"I'm always watching them. They're not moving. Butt Hair isn't supposed to use them during the regular school day."

"Yeah, because Butt Hair always does the right thing. I could've sworn I saw it zoom in. It didn't rotate, though."

It was nothing new. Buthaire was always watching me and for a guy who made sure everyone followed all of his stupid rules, he didn't seem to follow rules, either.

"Are you nervous about tonight?" Sophie asked. "Are you prepared?"

"A little. I've been writing my speech. I'll be ready tonight."

The School Board meeting was later that night. I was going to speak in front of them again. I had done so once before when Prince Butt Hair canceled the Halloween Dance because I wore a prison costume to school. It was epic. But still, I was nervous to do it again.

"But will they be ready for you?"

8

The School Board meeting was packed. Apparently, when I wasn't speaking, nobody showed up and they were a giant snore fest. I wondered if I should charge a speaking fee to cover my legal costs when Principal Buthaire finally got me expelled. After much drooling, it was time for the public comments. I was the only one who had signed up. I stood up in front of what looked like half the kids in our school and their parents, along with some teachers, Principal Buthaire, Ms. Pierre, and the entire Board of Education. I adjusted the microphone on the podium lower and cleared my throat. I wished there was something to do to catch the butterflies in my stomach or stop my heart from pounding so hard I could feel my big toe pulsing.

"You may remember me from last year when I asked you to reinstate the Halloween dance. Unfortunately, our principal has once again taken away the dance, this time from those who don't meet his flawed code of conduct, which is also scored with bias."

"Mr. Davenport, what evidence do you have of this?" the Board President asked.

"Well, I'm on the list," I said. He didn't get my joke.

"That's not good enough."

I looked over at Principal Buthaire, who was smiling ear to ear.

I continued, "You lose points based on who you spend time with."

"So, you're saying the program is allowed to penalize kids for being friends with certain children?"

"Yes, if you hang out with kids who rank poorly, you lose points. Is that what this school and this community are about? Excluding kids?" I asked.

"No, no I don't believe it is."

"And Principal Buthaire has also created a Peer Review Committee, which has certain students giving and taking away points from other students, a power that has been abused."

"I'd like to gather more information. Principal Buthaire, please step up to the microphone to answer questions from the Board."

Principal Buthaire walked toward me, his eyes locked on mine. I backed away from the podium, but didn't know if I should sit down.

"Our Student Behavior System is working very well. Austin has been a behavior problem since well before this system was implemented-"

The crowd erupted into boos and jeers.

"Liar!"

"You're a bully!"

"Your mustache is crooked!"

"Please calm down, everyone," the Board President said.

I looked into the crowd to see my mother, anything but

calm. I shook my head at her. I knew she was on the verge of rushing up to the stage and crushing Principal Butt Head with a Camel Clutch. In hindsight, I was disappointed I stopped her.

Principal Buthaire continued, "I can show you the detention records of his poor behavior. As far as the peer reviews, the students have been trained in the code of conduct, there are checklists for easy assessments, and everything is documented."

The Board President interjected, "Don't you think it's a problem to have students monitoring other students?"

"I understand your concern, but they are simple hall monitors and the rules are very clear. It's more of a service, helping kids get to class, making sure no one walks alone, and keeping everyone safe."

He was lying through his stupid mustache.

"Your mustache is crooked like the rest of you!"

"It's time to shave the Butt Hair!"

Principal Buthaire took a deep breath and forced a smile. "There's nothing wrong with the system. Ms. Pierre and I made sure it was supported by a strong foundation of research. If you recall, she went to Harvard."

The Board President and most of the others nodded, seemingly in agreement with Prince Butt Hair.

"Well, that may be, but there are clear shortcomings to the system. Discriminatory policies that penalize students simply because of who they are friends with will not stand in our community."

The crowd started to cheer.

The President continued, "That is not who we are, nor who we wish our children to be." He looked down the line at the rest of the Board members and said, "All in favor of striking that protocol from the Student Behavior System?"

The Board all answered, "Yes."

The crowd started to buzz. Some people were cheering. Others were clapping. But panic rushed through my veins. I rushed to the microphone and grabbed it before Principal Buthaire even knew what was happening.

"Sir, the whole system is a problem. The whole thing should be scrapped."

The crowd cheered.

"I understand your frustration, but sometimes kids just have to trust that the rules are there for a reason. We don't see a problem with the system, only that particular piece that was discriminatory. Thank you for bringing this matter to our attention. As for the Halloween dance, the administration has always reserved the right to grant access to school events based on behavior. We see no reason to change this. Good evening, everyone. This meeting is adjourned."

"When has half the school ever been banned for bad behavior?"

Nobody answered. The Board members gathered their things and quickly exited, the crowd growing restless.

Principal Buthaire whispered, "Nice try. Enjoy your evening in failure."

I stood there in stunned silence. Parents and kids were yelling from the crowd, most of them angry about the ruling, while some were still harping on Principal Buthaire's misshapen mustache.

9

Cheryl updated the Freedom Forum with news about the dance. We were not going to give up. She asked that everyone support freedom by wearing something red, which would make them all flouterers of the code. We didn't know who would join us, or if anyone would.

I walked into school, knowing Principal Buthaire was going to hit even harder. Randy and his Peer Review Committee would be emboldened to do just about anything they wanted. I had to figure something out before Nick DeRozan bought that hair buzzer, unless I wanted a bunch of hairless Zeroes walking around, which I most certainly did not. I was Zero number one. Confusing, I know, but sometimes the truth is.

My butt didn't even hit my seat in Advisory when the Speaker of Doom crackled. I knew it was for me before Mrs. Murphy even spoke.

"Adiós, muchacho," I said to Just Charles.

"Where are you going?"

I pointed to the Speaker of Doom.

Mrs. Muprhy's voice echoed through the Speaker of Doom, "Mrs. Callahan, please send Austin Davenport to the Principal's office. Immediately."

Mrs. Callahan looked at me with pity. "Stay strong, Austin. You're doing the right thing."

"Getting pummeled with detentions? Does Principal Buthaire think this is some kind of sport?"

I walked out to chuckles. I headed down to the main office, half expecting Ms. Pierre or Randy to give me a detention for being in the hallway. Surprisingly, I made it to Principal Buthaire's office without any resistance. I walked in, forced a smile at Mrs. Murphy, and slumped into my personal chair next to the copy machine.

Principal Butt Hair's voice called out from his office, "Send in the next victim, er, student."

Mrs. Murphy nodded at me. I stood up and walked into The Butt Crack. Principal Buthaire had both hands folded on his desk, waiting for me with a smirk.

"Good morning, sir. Since I spend so much time waiting in the office to see you, if you could find a few bucks to upgrade my chair, it would be greatly appreciated."

"Sit down, Misterrrrr Davenport."

I took that as a no.

Principal Butt Hair stared at me for a solid minute before he continued, "I just called you down here to smirk at you."

"Can I close my eyes until you're done?"

"Negatory. I was thinking about my victory last night. I can't take points from your friends just because they have bad taste, but I can be all over them like a duck on a june bug."

"I'm confused, sir."

Prince Butt Hair rolled his eyes. "I'll put it in terms you can understand. Like ketchup on a hot dog."

"Oh, okay." I like mustard better, but I got it. "I'll be sure to let them know."

"You think this is a game, Misterrrr Davenport?"

"No, sir."

"Then maybe you should quit playing around and fall in line. Now, be gone. I'm tired of smirking at you."

Me, too. I stood up and paused, waiting for him to give me a detention slip for existing. He was scanning papers on his desk, so I hightailed it out of there before he realized he hadn't detentioned me yet.

It was weird that Principal Buthaire let me go without giving me a late pass, but I figured it out soon enough. Ms. Pierre was waiting for me on the way to class.

"So, we meet again, Mister Davenport. I have a surprise for you," Ms. Pierre said with a twisted smile.

I knew it wasn't a Christmas morning kind of surprise. "Detention?" I asked.

She took a deep breath. "Principal Buthaire told me you would ruin everything."

She tore the detention sheet off and handed it to me. They made a great pair, evil as they were. The Detention Duo. The evil forces against me were multiplying. I already had two Randys to deal with, as I was volunteering at the retirement home with Malcolm and now I had two Butt Hairs to deal with. I didn't think middle school could get any worse than last year, but I was sorely mistaken.

∼

WE CALLED a team meeting after school. The Freedom Fighters met at Frank's Pizza, as usual. Ben called the meeting to order with a rap of the grated cheese on the table.

"Let the record show, the meeting began at 3:22," Ben said.

"We're keeping records?" Luke asked.

"That's not important," I said. "I think there's only one thing to talk about today. The system is broken and so, we must break it."

"I thought you said it was already broken," Ben said.

"Yeah, how do we break it if it's already broken?" Cheryl Van Snoogle-Something asked.

"Well, yes. It's already broken, but it's still in operation, so we have to break it."

"So, it's not broken," Sophie said.

I huffed. "It's a bad system. We need to stop it. The school board, the PTA, nobody is going to help us. Nerd Nation is at risk from terrorists and they must be stopped. We're on our own." It may have been a little dramatic, but can you blame me after everything we had been through?

"The Freedom Fighters need to take matters into our own hands," Just Charles said.

"Exactly," I added.

"But how?" Luke asked.

"We create our own system that counteracts the Student Behavior System and Butt Bucks."

"What, like getting points for doing the opposite of what Prince Butt Hair wants?" Sophie asked.

"Yes," I said, smiling. "Anybody who breaks the code of conduct or creates chaos, no, mayhem, will get points."

"Mayhem. I like the sound of that," Ben said.

"It has a nice ring to it, I agree," I said.

"What are we doing about the dance?" Sophie asked. "I still want to go with you," she said to me.

Cheryl said, "I heard it's going to be hard to get into the dance. I heard Randy talking about it. Everybody's name is going to be on a list, you need ID and there'll be a ton of security guards."

"Well, we'll have to find a way in anyway," I said.

"He was hoping you would try to sneak in. He said he was going to laugh as you got stomped," Cheryl said, shaking her head.

"Awesome," I said, tapping my chin.

"So how are we gonna sneak in?" Just Charles asked.

"It's gonna be impossible," Ben said.

"How many times have we done the impossible?" I asked.

Just Charles said, "Technically, never, because if we did it, it was possible."

"I'm talking about doing stuff we didn't think we could do."

"Oh, right. Yeah, a bunch! Like all the time, except for gym class. Most of that stuff is impossible," Just Charles said.

~

I SAT at the kitchen table doing homework after dinner. My mother walked in with a basket full of laundry.

"I've been meaning to ask you. How's the volunteering going at Vintage?"

"Ugh," I said. "It's so frustrating. They can't do anything. I'm just wheeling them around trying to find their dentures."

"That's the whole point. It's community service. You're there to help them."

"Well, I don't like it. One of the guys is like Randy but ninety."

Derek walked in and rifled through the laundry basket.

"Easy, I just folded all of that," my mother said. "What are you looking for?"

"This," Derek said with a smile, as he pulled out a football jersey. Oh, no. Mom, the stupid number on my favorite jersey is falling off."

"Which one is that?" my mother called out.

I looked at the jersey Derek held in his hands. It was black and white with the number twenty sewn onto the front.

"My favorite one. The Knights."

"Oh, that one is getting way too small. That can't fit you," she said.

"I'll wear it."

"Really?" my mother asked.

"I'm not giving this to him," Derek said, like his usual idiot self.

Just like any parent, my mother was all over the potential for a hand-me-down. Normally, I wanted my own stuff, but never got it. The opportunity to get me some free clothes without a fight was too good for my mother to pass up.

"I bought it for you, so if it doesn't fit you, and it doesn't, he's getting it if he wants it."

I smiled as I took it out of his hands. "It just needs some adjustments," I said to myself, smiling.

10

I needed to start working on my Halloween dance plan. Since the Board of Education ruled that we would not be allowed to go, there would be consequences. I didn't know what they were at that time, but my parents always instilled in me that there would be consequences, so it just sounded good.

How could I sneak past a fully-equipped security team? I had outsmarted them before when I snuck a selfie-stick into school when all non-educational items were banned, but it was going to be a lot harder to sneak in full-sized people. Just a tad. But that's when I thought of Goat Turd. I'm talking about the band, not the turd of an actual goat. I mean, really. I may tell fart jokes now and again, but how gross do you think I am?

I immediately emailed Cameron Quinn, lead singer of the band, Goat Turd. I got the band's email address from their website: Goatturd.com.

I wrote, "Cameron- it's Austin from Mayhem Mad Men. I need your help. If you're not on the road with the band, can you meet up at Burger Boys? If not, can we FaceTime?"

I had no idea how often the band checked their emails or if Cameron would even want to get back to me. He was super cool when we met him at Camp Cherriwacka and gave us a lot of great advice about being nerds and starting a band. Within a few minutes, he responded.

"Aus the Boss! Great to hear from you. I'll help any way I can. I could go for some Burger Boys. 6 P.M.?"

"Yes!" I pumped my fist.

I rushed into the den to find my dad. He was sitting on the couch, reading a novel.

"What's up, bud?"

"Can you take me to Burger Boys at six? I'm going to meet up with the lead singer of Goat Turd."

"A little collabo?"

"What's that?" I asked.

"Sorry, my rap game is not as strong as it used to be. People don't say collabo when two music groups collaborate on a new song?"

"No, I think your rap game needs work. I'm not certain it was ever strong."

"That hurts," he said with a smile.

"Sorry. And thanks."

∿

CAMERON QUINN WAS WAITING for me in a booth when I walked into Burger Boys. My dad headed over to a seat at the counter while I slipped into the booth across from Cameron.

"Yo, Aus," Cameron said, holding his fist out for a pound.

I pounded his fist and was grateful that he didn't ask for a high five. It was kind of my Kryptonite.

"Hey, man. Thanks for meeting with me. Congrats on the gig at our school."

"Oh, yeah. I mean, it's not up to our usual standard, but some of us are former Gophers, so we like to give back. And I think we're gonna try out some new songs. The Mayhem Mad Men are so good, I forget you're still in middle school."

"Thanks."

"So, what's up? What can I help with?"

"I think I can help you have a phenomenal show, but it might require sneaking in a few people under the radar, and some other theatrics. I may even write you a song."

"A collabo? Goat Turd and Mayhem Mad Men? I love it."

"You know what a collabo is?"

"Of course. I used to listen to rap. And I'm in. Anything for you, bro."

∾

I WALKED into school the next morning without a jacket, even though it was a chilly fall day. I wanted to show off my not-so-new, but much improved jersey that I got from Derek. I cut off the number two on the jersey, leaving the zero. True, it was a little bit off center, but the message was clear. I was a zero and I was proud of it.

As I navigated through the packed Atrium before Advisory, I got a bunch of fist bumps and high fives.

Jay Parnell gave me a hug. "Dude, you rocked it last night and I'm not talking about the Mad Men."

"Yeah, but we lost. Still no Halloween dance."

"You'll figure it out."

"Maybe," I said. I did have some good ideas, but there was still a lot to do and a lot to go right, and that wasn't always my specialty.

"Later, Aus," Jay said.

I walked over to Just Charles and Sammie, who were talking together. "Good morning, fellow Freedom Fighters."

"Nice shirt!" Just Charles said. "I'm getting one for tomorrow!"

"Thanks. I need to ask something big of you both."

"What is it?" Sammie asked.

"I have two questions for you. Do you believe in ghosts? And how do you feel about dying at the dance?"

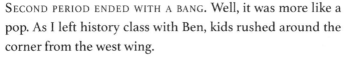

Second period ended with a bang. Well, it was more like a pop. As I left history class with Ben, kids rushed around the corner from the west wing.

Somebody yelled, "Stampede!"

Ben and I took off running in the same direction as the

crowd, with a mix of fear and excitement swirling in my chest. I imagined it was similar to the feeling that people got when they tried to outrun the bulls in Pamplona, Spain. Maybe to a lesser extent, though, because there were no actual bulls, but Nick DeRozan was close.

"Aww, what's that smell?" I yelled.

"It's disgusting!" Ben yelled.

"It's Cherry Avenue! It's always disgusting! This is so much worse than normal!"

I looked up ahead as we ran down the hallway. Zorch stood firm, the crowd streaming around him like he was a giant rock in the white-water rapids. He had a look in his eye like he was about to tame a dragon.

"Settle down," Zorch called out. "It's just a stink bomb. Nobody's dead…yet."

As we ran past Zorch, Luke caught up to us. He looked at me and smiled, "You owe me fifty points for this one!"

Oh, boy. What did I start?

~

THE SCHOOL HAD to be evacuated. 'Someone' set off a stink bomb in the ventilation system through a vent in the boys' bathroom (not Max's). As much as I appreciated the mayhem, because Prince Butt Hair was flat-out livid, Luke probably could've picked a better tactic. We had enough B.O. in the hallways. We didn't need to amplify it by a thousand.

Outside the school, I found Just Charles. "I got another question for you," I whispered.

"Not sure I want to know," he said, smiling.

"I haven't seen any of your magic shows lately. Do you still mess around with your magic kits and stuff?"

"No," he said, then whispered, "Well, yeah. A lot. I'm beyond kits, though. I don't do tricks anymore. I do illusions."

"I didn't know there was a difference."

"It's huge," Just Charles said, looking at me like I was an idiot.

"Yeah, okay. I guess this is bigger than tricks. We need an illusion. Can you make me disappear?"

"I'd rather saw you in half."

"Very funny. Can you?"

"Yes. Do we need anything else?"

"Pulleys. Wire from the theatre."

"Make sure your underwear doesn't show," Just Charles said, trying not to laugh and not doing a very good job of it. You may remember the time I flashed my Batman underwear to the entire audience at the Santukkah! musical.

"Very funny, but It's not for me. It's for Cameron Quinn. We also need two identical ghost or grim reaper costumes. Two Bluetooth speakers. And I think we're gonna need Zorch."

"Good luck with that one."

I know. It was gonna be a big ask.

11

I stayed after school that day. I needed to talk to Zorch. My plans for the Halloween dance were going to be very difficult to pull off without his help and nearly impossible if he was against us. After the final bell rang, I quickly grabbed my things from my locker and headed toward Zorch's lair. He usually hung out there until all the kids cleared out, before he started cleaning up the day's disaster of a mess.

I was one of the few students to ever enter Zorch's lair. Most kids were afraid of him. He was big and constantly at odds with kids who wore shirts about saving the environment, while throwing all their trash on the floor in the cafeteria. He and I were tight, though. He got me out of a few jams in my short time at Cherry Avenue, mainly problems that my brother caused, like Power Locking me and nearly taking my head off with a handful of beef stroganoff.

The door to Zorch's lair was open a crack. I knocked and pushed the door open a bit and peeked in.

"Who goes there?" Zorch asked.

"It's Austin."

"Oh, hey buddy. Come on in."

I opened the door and stepped inside.

"Have a seat," Zorch said, pointing to a chair across from the one he was seated in. He flipped a magazine onto his desk and looked at me. "Just move those blueprints onto the table."

"What are they for?" I liked building stuff, so blueprints were kinda cool.

"Just blueprints for the building. We're fixing a wall that had some water damage. This place is falling apart. So, what's up? You're not here to steal all my soap again, are you? The Halloween dance is right around the corner."

I chuckled. "No, I promise. This time, I'm going to ask for your help."

"Uh, oh. What are you gonna do? Or worse, want me to do?"

I smiled and thought for a moment. I knew he was only partially kidding. "Well, you may not be aware that many kids, me included, are not allowed to go to the dance because of Butt Hair's new Student Behavior System."

"I've heard. I was sorry to hear."

"Thanks. So, I tried to fix it by going to the Board of Education, but they support his decision. And even though the PTA sponsors it, they can't overrule the school on behavior issues. I've decided to give those kids who are allowed to go an...interesting Halloween experience. It's really just a bit of fun. I designed a performance with Goat Turd that I think people will really enjoy."

"Austin, I draw the line at bringing animal poop into my school. The stink bombs were bad enough. I don't need the real stuff here."

"Goat Turd is the band that's playing at the dance."

"Oh, right. So, what's the plan? There won't be any

pyrotechnics, right? Mayhem Mad Men didn't have much success with them over the summer."

"No, nothing like that. Super easy stuff. I just need a wire to attach to the lead singer so we can throw him against the wall when he's attacked by ghosts."

"Oh, just that?" Zorch laughed. Then his face got serious. "I can't help you..."

Disappointment enveloped me. I didn't blame him, but still I had big plans that were likely to fall flat, allowing Butt Hair to win. And I hated the thought of that.

Zorch continued, "But you should know that during the dance, they'll be a wire hanging from the rafters that you may see from the stage. Totally coincidentally."

I was so excited I nearly jumped out of my chair. "You're the best!"

"It's just a coincidence. No need to get crazy. Is that it?" Zorch asked with his fingers crossed.

"That's it. Why don't you have any questions for me?" I blurted out.

"I trust you."

"You do?"

"Mostly."

That was good enough for me. Plus, Mr. Muscalini always tells me how much insurance we have whenever I question the safety of the activity he had planned for us nerds. So, Zorch was probably good with that.

~

WITH MY MAJOR plans in place for the Halloween dance, I had a few additions I wanted to include. They would be devastating and very easy to execute. I walked into the kitchen. My dad was chowing down on a snack while reading something on his iPad.

"Dad, are you going to Costco any time soon?" I asked.

"Yeah, why?" he said, and looked up at me with a furrowed brow.

"I need some stuff for a science project."

"Like what?"

"A hundred onions."

"Okay."

"They probably have a bag of them for like $7, right?" I asked.

"I'll see what I can do."

A few hours later, my dad walked into the house with a bunch of stuff. He dumped a box onto the kitchen table and pulled something out. He tossed a bag in the air toward me. A huge bag of onions hurdled toward me like a cannon ball. I retrenched in fear as the bag of onions pummeled me and fell to the floor.

"Sorry," my dad said through his oops face.

I picked the bag up and checked out the onions.

"Nice catch. There are the onions you asked for."

Derek shook his head, "You're so weird, dude. What're you gonna do with them?"

"Stupid science stuff," I said, not wanting to give up any secrets.

"Yeah, I'm bored already."

Good.

～

IT WAS the night of the Halloween dance. I told my parents I was going to help Goat Turd with their performance that just so happened to be at the middle school dance that I had been banned from. It was a risk because Derek would be there, so after the mayhem ended, there was a good chance he'd blame me.

I crouched down in the back of the equipment van with Sophie, Sammie, Ben, and Just Charles. Ben and I wore matching grim reaper-like costumes. Sophie wore a matching black masquerade mask and dress, while Sammie wore a green outfit with a cape and mask, as if she was a female Robin Hood. Just Charles was full-on Spiderman. There were four empty equipment cases spread out across the floor.

"Are we really doing this?" Ben asked.

"If everyone's ready, we are," I said.

The rear door of the van creaked open. Cameron Quinn peeked in. "You sure you want to do this?"

"Never been so sure of anything in our whole lives," I said.

Just Charles scratched his head. "I'm not that certain, but I'm still in."

"Okay, there are holes drilled in the sides of these equipment containers. We'll get you in. What you do from there is up to you."

"Understood. Be gentle with me. I have a hundred caramel apples in mine."

"Ooh, can I have one?"

"What about your girlfriend?" Sophie asked. I wasn't sure if she was mad or joking.

"You want a caramel apple?"

"I meant about being gentle," she said, smirking.

"Oops. Cameron, please be extra gentle with Sophie's container. Very special cargo." I pointed to Ben. "You can roll his in if you want."

"Hey!"

"Alright, hop in," Cameron said.

We did as we were told and hopped into the containers.

"Good luck everyone. If this doesn't work, it's all Ben's fault. If it works, it was a team effort," I said.

"Yeah, right," Ben said.

I closed my container. Despite the air holes, it was pitch black. We lay there for a few minutes until the van door creaked open again. A lock clicked and a container scraped across the bottom of the van floor. Just Charles was locked and loaded. I wasn't sure that was what the term actually meant, but still, it fit.

Another lock and slide. And then another. A tap from the top of my container echoed inside. I held a large, covered tray of caramel apples on my chest that stretched down to my knees. I felt a jolt inside the container as someone tugged on the handle to my side.

I slid slowly across the van floor and then was jolted down as I heard two voices grunt, gravity taking hold. I was lowered gently to some sort of cart that squeaked and wobbled as I stabilized inside.

I heard a man's voice say, "What's in there?"

Cameron said, "We're the band. Goat Turd."

The voice said, "I heard you guys stink."

"Yeah, good one," Cameron said, forcing a laugh.

"No, really."

"We won Battle of the Bands two years ago."

"Right, must've been 64 Farts I was thinking of."

"Yep, they stink," Cameron said.

"That's a lot of equipment," Ms. Pierre's voice said.

I tried to peek out of the air holes, but I couldn't see anything.

Cameron stammered, "Well, you know, we're a big band and we're gonna rock this place tonight."

"Not too loud, okay?" Ms. Pierre said, then asked, "Have you seen this child?"

"Aus-" Cameron stopped abruptly. 'Umm, I'm lost. Who is he?"

"He's a hoodlum. Steer clear of him. If you see him, though, please alert security immediately."

"I most certainly will."

12

I was wheeled inside. There were a lot more bumps than I remembered, getting up ramps and over door thresholds. I was bouncing around like I was on a trampoline. I almost groaned a few times after my backbone slammed into the container. After an oversized bump, the caramel apple container popped open and a few squeezed out, one of which attached to my head. I plucked it off and held it in my hand. I could feel the caramel on my face. I should've put my mask on before we went in, but I was afraid of not getting enough air. After a few minutes of wheeling, we stopped and sat still for at least ten minutes. I was getting hungry. I almost starting eating the caramel apple, which, if you've been paying attention, you've probably figured out that they were not really apples.

After another few minutes, Cameron said, "Here we go." A machine started whirring. "Let's just test this fog machine out. It was a little shaky last time we used it."

The lock clicked open and then the lid of the container flipped off. The container quickly filled with fog.

Cameron whispered, "Stay low and head straight back to

the girl's locker room. The rest of the crew will meet you there."

Great. That wasn't the plan. All I needed was for Principal Buthaire to catch me in the girl's locker room. It would be an immediate expellment (is that a word?) and enrollment at LaSalle Military Academy, a boarding school that specializes in the crushing of misunderstood boys' souls for profit.

"Take the apples," I whispered to Cameron.

"Oh, right." Cameron reached inside my container and removed the caramel apples.

I climbed over the side and fell to my knees on the floor. I swallowed my pain. I army crawled my way to the girls' locker room, perhaps practicing for my banishment to LaSalle. I could see through the fog that the door was already open, so even though it hurt, I hustled across the hard gym floor to safety.

I entered the girls' locker room and crawled around the corner to safety. I heard whispering coming from a group of lockers. I followed it. As I got closer, I held my hand out in front of me, still not able to see from the fog that had filled up the lower half of the locker room. I kept moving forward until I came to an abrupt stop, bumping heads with someone.

"Oww!" I said, reflexively.

"Shhh," Sammie whispered, only a few inches from my face.

"Who's here?" I whispered.

"Me and Ben. Sophie and Just Charles are probably a few minutes behind."

Sophie and Just Charles made it without a problem.

"We should go back toward the office," Sophie said. "There's a little alcove back there where we can hide. Follow me."

We made it to the alcove. I stood up and was actually able to see everyone above the fog. It hovered around our waists.

"What are you wearing?" Sophie asked me.

"My costume?"

"No, these." Sophie removed two caramel apples that were sticking to my costume.

"Oooh, that looks good," Just Charles said. He grabbed it and bit into it before I was able to stop him.

"No-"

At first, I thought he would be okay, but he quickly spit it out. "Yuck! That was disgusting. That's the worst apple I've ever tasted."

"That's because it's not an apple," I said. "Sorry. Forgot to tell you. But you probably should've realized I wasn't bringing snacks for the rest of the school. Well, I'm glad I made a lot. Costco's a life saver."

"What did you do?" Just Charles asked.

"I dipped like a hundred onions in caramel and red food coloring and I'm gonna put them out on the food tray once everyone shows up."

"That's not right, bro," he said, wiping his mouth.

"Yeah, but it's gonna be so right when Randy bites into one and cries like a baby in front of Regan."

~

THE DANCE WAS STARTING. It was time to make an exit from the girls' locker room. Sophie led the way. I followed behind her, looking around to make sure Principal Butt Hair or Ms. Pierre wasn't lurking in the dark corners of the girls' locker room. My esteemed principal already accused me once of breaking into the girls' locker room and stealing underwear. For the record, it was not true.

"Walk like a girl," she said.

"What does that mean?" I asked.

"Talk like a girl, too."

"I'm just gonna be a mute."

"Yeah, because we have so many mutes walking around Cherry Avenue that you could be confused with."

"Fair point," I said, in my highest pitched voice.

We all walked in different directions once we exited the girls' locker room. I headed over to the stage where Cameron and the crew were starting to warm up. There were dozens of students walking around the gym, trying to find places to hang out and look cool. I still had work to do. I loitered past the stage and around the side toward a bunch of equipment off to the side. I reached into a bin, grabbed the air horn that was waiting for me, and slipped it into my pocket.

I walked over to the boys' locker room, looked around to make sure no one in a position of authority was watching, and slipped in. It was perfect timing, as I saw Principal Buthaire out of the corner of my eye, heading toward me. He led a group of security guards around the outer edge of the gym.

As I taped the air horn to the back of the door, I heard Principal Buthaire speaking. I froze.

"Be on the lookout for hooligans. If anyone sees that trouble maker, Austin Davenport, you are to swarm like killer bees. Do you understand?" Principal Buthaire whined.

I stood behind the door, waiting for them to move on. After a few minutes without hearing Prince Butt Hair's stupid face talking, I cracked open the door and peeked out. I didn't see him anywhere and it looked like the dance was starting to pick up.

I slipped out from behind the door and hurried over to the band where a bunch of kids had started to congregate. I needed to blend in and stay away from Ben, who was wearing the exact same costume as I was.

All the idiots were there. Randy, Regan, Derek, Jayden, Nick, and a whole bunch of their followers were there, ruining the dance that I was about to ruin. And my plan was working like a charm. As soon as Cameron slipped over to the food table and slid the apples onto the table, the kids swarmed to them like they were giant sugar magnets.

I watched them and prayed that they would each devour them like mad, but no. Randy shook his head. Figures. What kind of kid doesn't like candy? Randy was the worst of the worst. And then Regan took a bite and forced it into Randy's face. He looked at it funny. I was concerned that he had figured it out. But he was just trying to figure out how to eat it properly and without getting messy.

Randy took a bite and immediately regretted it. Regan had already spit out her bite and was wiping her mouth, confused as to what had just gone so horribly wrong.

Derek was such a doofus. While Randy and Regan were busy crying, spitting, and complaining, he grabbed an apple and sunk his teeth in. I think I got the most satisfaction at watching him cry his eyes out and hurl into the garbage pail.

Dozens of kids were running in all different directions. They were knocking each other over to get to the garbage pails. Other kids went straight for the locker room bathrooms. One by one, they burst through the bathroom doors and were met with an air horn blast that rattled their brains. It was glorious.

Once everything settled down, Goat Turd kicked it off. I slipped away. I had to haunt the dance in just a few minutes. Just Charles had taught me the illusion I needed. I hoped it would work.

As I got situated on the ledge above the gym, Cameron spoke into the microphone, "Here's a new song called, 'Conformity.' It was written by a good friend."

I positioned the Bluetooth speaker around my neck. Sophie would be streaming to it from down below. I hadn't seen her in a while. It was by design, but still I hoped that everything was a go. Nobody would know what was going on or even know that I was there since I stood in a black costume without being able to speak.

The music kicked off and Cameron went straight into the song. "Be yourself. Don't get in line to be like everybody else! Be free! Forget conformity."

His dance moves were exquisite, as always. The girls were surrounding the small stage, cheering like crazy.

Cameron was busy high fiving the crowd before the next verse.

"Let me hear you shout, I wanna stand out! Break the mold, don't do what you're told! Conformity...is not for me!"

I stood up at the top of the rafters, looking down on the dance. It was time.

13

My heart was pounding, as I watched the kids below me dance around the stage. As soon as the lights flickered, it was on.

All of the room's attention was on Cameron Quinn. He continued the song I wrote, "Conformity...it's not for-"

The lights flickered. Cameron Quinn looked up at me, a silouhette in the window, the moon lighting the platform around me.

"What is that thing?" Cameron said, his voice shaking.

The speaker on my chest, which I dubbed the Speaker of Ghoul, reverberated against my chest as the recording played, "Ha ha ha. I'm the ghost of Mr. Jenkins! It's been twenty years since my death."

"You're not real. You're just trying to spook us!" Cameron yelled.

"Silence, turd boy!"

I thrust my hand toward Cameron. Cameron surged into the air, slammed into the wall, and hovered there, suspended over the speakers on the stage.

The crowd shrieked. Nobody seemed to know what to do.

Just Charles yelled in his deepest voice, "It's just a kid in a costume!"

I thrust my hand toward Just Charles. Sammie's timing was impeccable. She tossed one of Just Charles' magic smoke bombs at his feet. It popped with a flash of light.

Purple smoke smoldered around Just Charles' body that lay motionless on the floor.

Some people started running. Other people looked up on the ledge for me, but I was gone.

"Where did he go?" people asked, frantically.

Ben jumped out from behind the crowd, wearing the exact same costume as I was. His Speaker of Ghoul blasted, "Looking for me?" It was followed by an evil cackle that was ten times worse than Principal Buthaire's ever was.

Sammie ran toward the exit, passing Ben by only a few feet. Ben thrust his palm at her. She dropped a magic smoke bomb, then fell to the floor. Shrieks and smoke surged all around Sammie. Mayhem was ensuing everywhere as the gym emptied.

My crew rushed out the back door of the gym and disappeared into the night.

14

Everyone at the bus stop was talking about the Halloween dance. Even kids who weren't allowed to attend due to their Zero status, claimed to have been there and almost died, too. I was pretty sure that Goat Turd hadn't sneaked in anyone besides my crew and security was pretty tight, so I knew they were full of it.

Things got even crazier once we were on the bus. As we approached Cherry Avenue Middle School, I looked out the window to see a huge crowd and a Channel 2 News crew.

I smacked Ben on the arm. "Dude, I think Calvin Conklin is on site. Buthaire is gonna be all over me like a june bug on..."

"What?"

"Something. I can't remember. There were ducks and bugs. I don't know."

"Log into the TV app. Maybe we can watch it live."

"Good call, Gordo."

"Only Mr. Muscalini is allowed to call me that. I don't really like it, but his biceps are too big to put up a fight."

"It was kind of growing on me," I said, as I pulled out my phone and logged in. I popped on Channel 2 News. Calvin Conklin filled my screen.

Calvin looked at us and said, "Prank or paranormal? I'll let you decide." The camera panned out, revealing Matt Carrillo, an obnoxious motormouth. Calvin continued, "What did you see?" He held the microphone out in front of Matt's face.

Matt looked into the camera and started speaking like he just chugged seven cups of coffee. "One minute there was a ghost floating above us and the next minute, he vanished and reappeared behind us. He shot lightning bolts out of his palms and blasted two kids."

Calvin pulled the microphone back and held it up to his mouth. The camera zoomed in on him.

A squeaky voice called out, "We need to put an end to this nonsense now!" It was Buthaire!

Our bus pulled into the parking lot and rolled to a stop. We continued watching.

The camera panned out again, revealing Prince Butt Hair looking quite perturbed.

"Do you know the whereabouts of the two injured children?"

"There were no injured children. It was a prank."

"Anyone reported missing?"

"No, and we don't expect any."

"That sounds fishy and I'm a lot better looking than I am smart. I mean, it's not even close." Calvin looked into the camera and winked.

"There is nothing to see here," Principal Buthaire said. "Please pack up your belongings and let us get back to educating children."

Calvin looked at Principal Buthaire and paused thought-fully. "Strong mustache. I love a good 'stache, don't you? Who are you again?"

Principal Buthaire pursed his lips. A vein throbbed on his forehead. Even I had never made him that angry. He said through gritted teeth, "There was no paranormal activity here. We were the victims of a heinous prank. And I'm going to get to the bottom of this and punish those responsible."

"What about the two dead kids?"

"There were no dead children. That is preposterous."

"Are there any suspects?"

"Oh, you can bet on it." Principal Buthaire stared into the camera. It was his death stare that he reserved for giving me a detention. Ahh, farts.

"Are you sure there was no crime?"

"Not yet."

"How much do you want to bet?"

Prince Butt Hair walked away, shaking his head.

Calvin looked into the camera. "A murder mystery at Cherry Avenue Middle School. So exciting. Calvin Conklin signing off. Back to you, Fred, er Ned. Ted. Back to you, Ted."

15

The Freedom Fighters had an impromptu meeting in the Atrium. Everyone was a little regretful over creating so much chaos and a lot nervous about how Principal Buthaire would respond.

"The news is here," Sammie whispered through gritted teeth.

"I've always wanted to meet Calvin Conklin," Cheryl Van Snoogle-Something said, excitedly. "He's so handsome."

"He's such an idiot," Just Charles said, annoyed.

"Guys, it's gonna be okay. They can't prove anything. They don't know any of us were even there. We all stayed home in misery because we were left out of the dance."

"You think Butt Hair is gonna be okay with that?" Sophie asked.

"No, I'm sure I'll get summoned by the Speaker of Doom first thing."

And I was right. The Speaker of Doom crackled and Mrs. Murphy called me down. She immediately escorted me into The Butt Crack. I didn't even get to chill in my least favorite chair. It was serious if he didn't at least make me wait a little bit.

Principal Buthaire was standing up in front of a cork board. There were pictures of the dance, Goat Turd, me, and my crew, all seemingly taken from the school's security cameras last year. I was, of course, in the middle of the board with push pins and string running in every direction, as if he was trying to figure out how the dance debacle was tied to me.

He turned and stared at me as I stood before him. Principal Buthaire clapped slowly. I didn't say or do anything.

"Do you know why I'm clapping, Misterrrrrr Davenport?"

"You're going to pretend I did something good and then you're going to flip it like a beef patty at Burger Boys and give me detention and take a way a thousand Butt, er Buthaire Bucks from me?"

His face dropped like I just spoiled another Christmas surprise. "You got lucky on that, Misterrrr Davenport. But you're not lucky enough to avoid my evil, er sinister, er my wrath. Ms. Pierre is already checking the security tapes as we speak and I've given your name to the police. Confess now and I'll call off the detectives. The chief and I are close, personal friends."

I never met the police chief, but I immediately questioned his taste in humanity, if Principal Buthaire was even telling the truth. "Sir, if you recall, I wasn't allowed to go to the dance."

"As if the rules have stopped you before. You parade around here as if the rules don't even exist."

"Ok. Check your tapes. I never walked through those doors."

"Ha ha! I caught you! How did you know we let people in

through the doors?" Principal Butt Hair yelled while pointing his finger at me.

"Did you let anyone in through the windows?"

"Well, no," he said, disappointed again.

"Then unless Mr. Gifford finally completed his teleporter, I don't see how I could've done what you're accusing me of."

"He's working on a teleporter? Hopefully not on school time. I'm going to dock his pay, just in case," Principal Buthaire said, while jotting down a note.

I decided to go along with it. "Yes, he calls it the People-Porter. Until now, he's only been able to transport small rodents. His cat didn't make it." I looked down at the floor. "Schrodinger never had a chance...Or was it Beeker?"

I looked down at the ground in mourning.

"We'll be in touch once we have the evidence we're looking for."

Wonderful. Even though I didn't think they could prove anything, I was still nervous. I didn't know if Prince Butt Hair was telling the truth about the police, but if he was, I could get in a ton of trouble. And it would be my fault if my friends or Goat Turd got caught up in it.

～

I CALLED Cameron as soon as I got home from school. Derek was still at football practice, so I could talk about the dance without getting myself into trouble.

"Hey, it's Austin. I have some bad news," I said.

"Hey, Austin! How's it going, man?" Cameron asked, excitedly. "I'm having a spectacular day!"

I took a deep breath. I was about to ruin it. "Well, I'm sorry, but I have some bad news. My principal says the police are investigating what went down at the Halloween dance. It's all my fault."

"Hey man, no worries!"

"Really? You're not upset?"

"I've never been happier! Somebody videotaped Goat Turd during the concert and it went viral. We're gonna be huge!"

"Wow," I said, dumbfounded, which didn't happen often. "I'm shocked."

"Don't worry. Your secret is safe with me. Maybe the Mayhem Mad Men will join us on tour!"

"Yeah, that would be awesome," I said, my mind on the problem that had just popped into my head. There was video footage.

Cameron continued, "There were rumors going around on the Internet that I was dead."

"I'm so sorry, Cameron." I didn't know how to fix that.

"No, it was awesome. I mean, once my mother calmed down. But it's been great. We're booking gigs left and right!"

"That's really awesome. I'm happy for you. I'm sure you're busy with all that, so I'll let you get back to it. Just wanted to warn you about the cops."

"Not sweatin' it, bro. Talk to you soon! And thanks again!"

"No problem," I said, as I hung up the phone.

But I had a problem. There was video footage of Cameron being attacked and perhaps a whole lot more. I immediately pulled up YouTube and searched for the video. It was trending, so it wasn't hard.

Cameron was right. It went viral with over a million views. I didn't really care about that. I mean, I was happy for them, but that's not why I was checking it out. I clicked on the video. After the stupid advertisement, Goat Turd's performance kicked in. I didn't really care how the performance went or how they sounded. I was just looking for evidence. I wanted to make sure that the video didn't show anyone in our group, at least our faces, or the wire that Zorch had set up for us.

I watched the entire video five times, stopping, rewinding, and re-watching Cameron move around the stage with the wire attached, fly through the air and slam into the wall. I wasn't an expert, but it was dark enough that it looked real. I exhaled. Principal Buthaire likely wouldn't see any issues, if he even knew the video existed.

16

I was scheduled to spend an afternoon at Vintage Retirement Community. Lucky me. I was paired up with my old buddy, Malcolm. Another win. Oh, and Randy was there with Carl. Malcolm was sitting in a wheelchair in the community room, watching TV. I walked over and stopped beside him. I turned my back on Randy, hoping he wouldn't see me there.

"Hi there, Mr. Jabberwocky. Remember me?"

"Yeah, you're that kid who stinks at checkers, right? Alvin?"

"Austin," I corrected him, frustrated.

"You remind me of my grandson when he was your age, Alvin."

I took a deep breath. It was going to be a long two hours.

Malcolm continued, "He stunk at checkers, too. Maybe that's why he stopped coming around. I beat his butt too bad."

"Maybe," I said, doubting it.

"I'll try to take it easy on you," Malcolm said, with a toothless smile.

"Thanks, I appreciate that," I said. I thought about calling him out on his cheating, but he was like a hundred years old, so I just let it go. "What do you want to do today?"

"I need to find my dentures."

"Okay, but what do you want to do with me? You want to wheel out by the pool or the fountains?"

"I want to find my dentures," Malcolm said, grumpily.

Just great. We were going on a denture hunt.

"Where did you have them last?"

"If I knew that, Alvin, I wouldn't be missing them!"

I tried to keep my composure, but I wasn't sure if I was. "Where would you like to start looking?"

"Over by the ladies," Malcolm said, with a smile.

I chuckled. "Oh, so you think you lost your dentures by the ladies?"

"No, but that's where I'd like to start."

"Okay," I said. I wheeled Malcolm over to a small circle of women playing cards by the window.

We sat there for about ten minutes. I looked under the table and around the window ledges, while Malcolm stared at the old ladies while they played hearts. I really felt good about this community service I was providing. I was bored out of my skull.

"Hey, Malcolm. No dentures here. Where should we look next?"

"Maybe in my room. Let's check there."

As I turned Malcolm's wheelchair around, Randy and Carl were right behind us.

"Davenfart, did I hear you mention dentures?" He didn't wait for an answer. "Remember when you made out with that old lady at the concert? Her dentures ended up in your mouth, didn't they?"

"I didn't make out with her, idiot."

Carl and Malcolm were laughing.

"But her dentures were in your mouth, right?"

"This was at the Battle of the Bands that I won and you lost, right?" I asked, angrily.

"Oooh, burned," Carl said.

"Shut it, Carl," Randy said.

I turned away from Randy and wheeled Malcolm in a different direction. I was a lot more interested in going denture hunting with Randy around.

"How old was she?" Malcolm asked.

"Who?"

"The old lady you made out with."

"I didn't make out with any old ladies!"

"Maybe I could write her a letter?"

"People don't write letters anymore. And I don't know who she is," I said with a huff.

I wheeled Malcolm down the hall, navigating around other wheelchairs, people with walkers and canes, and a host of old people pile-ups.

"It's the next one on the left," Malcolm said.

"Okay," I said, backing into the doorway and opening it.

I wheeled into the studio apartment and looked around. It was nice enough and reasonably clean. There were pictures around of what looked like his kids and grandkids, maybe even great grandkids.

"Alvin, did I ever tell you that you remind me of my grandson when he was your age?"

"You did."

"He's right there," Malcolm said, pointing at a giant family picture on the way.

"The one with the mustache?" I asked. The dude was like sixty years old. I didn't see the resemblance.

"No, next to him," Malcolm said.

"Oh," I said, examining the picture. There was a dude only forty years old. With a goatee.

"You look just like him. Wish he came around more."

"So where are we gonna look for these dentures?" I asked.

"Well, I took them out when I was kissing Beatrice. Or was it Mary Alice? But I put them back in. And then took them out to kiss Mary Alice. Or was it Beatrice?"

The rest of my time went a lot like that. We never found Malcolm's dentures, but I did get a long list of women he either had kissed or wanted to kiss. It was not what I signed up for.

∾

THE NEXT DAY at school was interesting. I sat at lunch with Sophie, Sammie, and Just Charles. Ben walked over quickly, his eyes darting in every direction. He slipped into his seat and exhaled.

"Is it done?" I asked.

Ben smiled. "You know it."

"No, that's why I asked."

"Oh, yeah. It's done."

"What did you do?" Sophie asked.

"When Jared Leonard started haggling over how many pieces of bacon he was getting on his bacon sandwich, I dumped a bunch of cayenne pepper in the tomato bisque."

"That's gonna be a good one," Just Charles said. "You usually can't go wrong with the tomato bisque."

"Let's be honest," Sophie said. "There's nothing in this cafeteria that can't go wrong."

"Thanks for the reminder," I said. As I was checking my

Beef Ghoulash (hey, it was Halloween time) for safety hazards, Jay Parnell walked over.

He leaned in and whispered, "I want in, Davenport."

"To what? The Ghoulash? You might lose your hair. It's probably radioactive."

"Nah, man. To the group."

"You play an instrument?"

"Not your band. The secret group."

"I can't confirm or deny the existence of any secret group."

"I hear you, man. So, when do we meet?"

"I exhaled, frustrated. I'll let you know."

"There are others who want to join. Want to wreak havoc like you're wreaking," Jay said.

"It's mayhem. We're wreaking mayhem," I said, annoyed. Sophie looked at me, her eyes bulging. "That is, if there was an actual secret group."

Jay smiled and nodded, "Later."

Sophie said, "Why does everyone think you're always the one causing trouble?"

"Prince Butt Hair created a monster," Ben said.

I shook my head. "For a secret group, a lot of people sure know about it."

"Well, they know somebody is doing it. And you're the first one everybody thinks of. You kinda have a history," Sammie said. "Take it as a compliment."

"Luke says that Jasmine Jane wants to join," Just Charles said.

"Ugh."

Mr. Muscalini walked by and smiled. "Gentlemen, Gordo, ladies. Enjoy your lunch. I know I will. It's not every day you can have your veggies in your soup."

My eyes widened.

"What's the matter, Davenport?"

"Umm, nothing sir. It's just that, well, tomato is a fruit, not a vegetable."

Mr. Muscalini looked at his soup with hatred. "Dang it! That's totally gonna mess with my macros."

"What the heck is a macro?" Ben asked.

"So much to learn, fellas. So much to learn." Mr. Muscalini walked away.

"We probably should've warned some of the teachers not to eat the soup," I said.

I, of course, was right. We all looked over to see Mr. Muscalini's face morph deeper and deeper shades of red as he let out a primal scream.

"Bring the pain! I love the pain!" Mr. Muscalini wretched and grabbed his stomach. "I can't handle the pain!" he yelled, as he sprinted toward the condiment stand, barreling over poor Mrs. Winslow and Blake Peralta.

Mr. Muscalini grabbed the ridiculously oversized jug of mayo and tore out the pump atop it without unscrewing it and started chugging it. Mayo is not a fast-moving condiment, so he thrust his hand into the jar and started shoveling gobs of mayo into his mouth, hand after hand. His face slowly morphed back to its normal shade.

He exhaled, relieved that his insides were no longer on fire, and then hit the deck. Mr. Muscalini ripped off so many aerial pushups, lifting his entire body off the ground and clapping his hands before landing again, that I couldn't even count. The bell rang, so we left him to his workout.

17

After lunch, I walked with Sophie to the east wing. As we passed the teachers' lounge, I did a double take as I heard student voices inside. That was a huge no no. Students did not go in the teachers' lounge under penalty of death. Well, I didn't know that for sure, but that's kind of the way the teachers acted. The door was open, so we peeked in. It was usually closed. The teachers wanted no intruders. They probably had locks and chains on the other side, too.

"What's going on in there?" Sophie asked.

"I've never seen that door open. Oh, my God," I said.

Randy Warblemacher, leader of the Peer Review Council, sat on a couch, playing video games, while other kids ate lunch and socialized.

"They've been given the rights to the teachers' lounge. Unbelievable," Sophie said.

Dr. Dinkledorf walked up to Sophie and me, shaking his head.

"Sir, what is going on?" I asked.

"Our esteemed principal has let the Peer Review Committee dorks run amok. Amok!"

I didn't know what that meant, but it seemed pretty bad.

Dr. Dinkledorf continued, "I've had my lunch in that break room for more than forty years. I'm not gonna stop now just because some doofus of a principal comes up with some hair-brained scheme. Principal Puma was a pushover, but he was a billion times better than having Butt Hair, er, Prinicapal Butt- Buthaire."

"It's okay, sir. You don't have to pretend with us," I said.

"Good luck, sir," Sophie said, smiling.

"Good day. See you in class." Dr. Dinkledorf took a deep

breath and straightened his jacket. He walked into the room formerly known as the teachers' lounge.

"Warblemacher, sit up like a human being and move all these wires. You're gonna kill someone."

∼

AFTER SCHOOL, the Freedom Fighters assembled in the Atrium before the buses left.

Sophie asked me, "Did you tell them about the teachers' lounge?"

"Yeah. I'm so tired of those Peer Review Counselor rats," I said.

"So, what's next?" Ben asked.

"Why do you call them rats?" Sophie asked me.

"Because they rat us out to Butt Hair for Butt Bucks. Rats."

"So, what's next?" Ben asked, annoyed.

"I just told you. Rats."

"Rats?" Sophie asked, her eyes bulging.

"That sounds disgusting," Luke said.

"I was thinking we could drop a few rats into the new lounge," I said.

"Ooh, is that too much?" Sammie asked.

"Did you hear that Regan gave five hundred Butt Bucks to her friends for being prettier than everyone else?" I asked.

"Or Randy took away all of Blake Goldmartin's Butt Bucks because he didn't do Nick DeRozan's homework?" Ben added.

Sophie gritted her teeth. "Rats!"

I looked at Just Charles. "That's my girl."

Ditzy Dayna walked over and joined the group. "Hey

guys!" She looked at Sammie and said, "We're gonna be late for practice."

"In a minute," Sammie said.

Ditzy Dayna wasn't in our group per se, but she was friends with Sophie and Sammie, and probably wouldn't have any idea what we were talking about or remember any of it, anyway.

"Where the heck are we gonna get rats?" Just Charles asked.

I thought for a minute and then said, "What's the reptile kid's name that lives down the street from you, Luke?"

"Oh, God, no. He thinks he's a long-lost descendent of Salazar Slytherin. He talks to snakes and stuff."

"Slytherin, like from Harry Potter?" Ditzy Dayna asked.

"How many other Slytherins do you know?" Just Charles asked.

"Like four or five."

"Do you know any Ravenclaws?" Ben asked.

"That would be ridiculous."

I ignored her answer and looked at Luke. "That's exactly who we need. Can you make an introduction?"

"No."

"Really?"

"Dude, he's so weird."

"Maybe we just need to get to know him better," Ben said.

"He talks to snakes," Luke pleaded.

"So did Harry Potter," Sophie said, smiling. "Maybe he's the Chosen One."

"Yeah, the Chosen Weird One."

I looked at Luke and said, "Hey man, you're the weird one in this group and we still hang out with you."

"Me? I thought it was Ben?" Luke threw his hands up.

"It's totally you."

Sophie leaned in. "Honestly, none of you stand out that much."

"Thanks," I said, sarcastically.

"I meant that you're a good weird. More like unique."

Luke said, "The Slytherin kid is not the good weird, but he is extremely unique..."

~

THE SITUATION WITH THE FORMER TEACHERS' lounge deteriorated further the next day. Dr. Dinkledorf entered the cafeteria and sat down with some of the other teachers to eat. They were a few tables away from where we were sitting. What little hair he had left was wild and out of place, which was not the norm for him, and he looked worn down and unhappy.

As I passed by the teachers' table to grab a spork (an under-appreciated piece of flatware- half spoon, half fork), I asked him, "How did it go in the lounge, sir?"

Dr. Dinkledorf looked up at me with bloodshot eyes. "They're savages. Savages, I tell you. Nick DeRozan ate twelve moon pies on a dare. And then ate four more after it was over, just because!"

"I once ate twenty of those," Mr. Muscalini said. It was not overly helpful.

All of the teachers there were shaking their heads.

"Who eats moon pies anymore, anyway?" Dr. Dinkledorf said, exasperated.

"Exactly, sir. Exactly." I really had no idea what he was talking about, but I thought he just needed some support right about then.

18

I texted my mom and told her I was taking Luke's bus home. We had a project to complete. True, it was not a school project and it certainly wasn't a project she would approve of. Or maybe she would. She was tired of Principal Buthaire and all of his nonsense, like most of us were.

I sat with Luke, huddled next to him, waiting for the right moment. Sal sat alone in the seat across from us, staring out the window.

I nudged Luke, "Just talk to him."

"No, you."

"He's your friend."

"He's not my friend."

"You said you would do it."

"Okay," Luke said, defeated. He took a deep breath and leaned over toward Sal's seat. "Hey, Sal?"

Sal turned and looked at us, not sure why anyone was speaking to him. He said simply, "No, I'm not going to charm snakes at your birthday party. They're not some cheap parlor trick. They're not here to entertain you."

"Okay, well that was just my first question," Luke said. "My second question is about rats. Snakes eat them, right?"

"They're the filet mignon of the reptile world."

"That's good to know," I said. I looked at Luke, "I always wondered that. How about you?"

"Often." Luke looked back at Sal. "Where do you get them?"

"The Reptile Den, most of the time. I also import them from Russia. I've got a black market hook-up. They're half price, but harder to get. Do you need some?"

"Yeah, we're thinking about it," Luke said.

Sal furrowed his brow. "How many do you need?"

Luke looked at me. I said, "I don't know. A couple."

"Will they be put in harm's way?"

"We're going to put them in the teacher's lounge," Luke said. "Well, the Peer Review Counselors' lounge. I don't know what's going to happen to them from there."

"Don't you feed rats to your snakes?" I asked.

"Yeah."

"So why do you care what happens to them?"

"I was just curious because you two seem much more like hamster people."

I had never really thought about it, but I was pretty certain he was right. Because I knew like heck I wasn't a rat or snake person.

Sal continued, "And hamster people wouldn't hurt rats."

Luke said to me, "He's a wealth of rodent knowledge."

"Yes, I'm impressed," I said and then whispered, "and totally freaked out."

Luke asked, "Do rats like terrorizing?"

"They live for it, well, and for being eaten by snakes. Rats are highly intelligent creatures. What makes you think they'll listen to you and do what you want?"

I hadn't really thought about it. "We were just gonna drop them into a window or something. It's not going to be complicated."

"I could speak to them on your behalf," he said, eagerly.

"Yes, please do. I want to make sure they're on board with what we're doing," I said.

"When do you want 'em?"

"As soon as possible," I said.

Luke asked, "How much do they cost?"

"If it's to take down the Peer Review Counselors, they're on me." Sal looked at me. "My score on the zero board is so low, it's almost as bad as yours, hamster boy. And that's saying something."

"It sure is."

19

Sophie, Ben, and I had two hours to complete at Vintage. I still wasn't a fan, but Randy had a late practice, so at least he wouldn't be there. The three of us sat outside with Ethel and Charlie on benches, and Malcolm and Carl in wheelchairs. It was pretty boring. Although Carl's eyebrows were so bushy and mesmerizing, I wasn't sure if I had been staring into them for hours or days.

Malcolm broke a prolonged silence. "You wanna see my scars?"

Sophie turned up her nose. Ben shrugged.

I asked, "Whatcha got?"

Malcolm rolled up his sleeve, revealing a shriveled-up forearm that had a zig zag of a scar from his wrist to his elbow. "This is the tiger bite I got when I worked in the circus."

"You got bitten by a tiger?" Ben asked, his eyes bulging.

"Here he goes with the tiger story," Ethel said, rolling her eyes.

"You worked in a circus?" I asked. "I almost joined last year."

Sophie and Ben looked at me and frowned.

"It's a long story," I said. It was a rather low point in my life.

Malcolm looked at Ethel and said, "I saved a girl's life!"

"Show 'em the tattoos, Malcolm," Carl said, excitedly. He looked at Charlie. They both stifled laughs.

Malcolm did some maneuvering in his robe and eventually revealed his shoulder.

I looked at the tattoo. It looked like my brother's chin. It was a giant butt.

"You got a tattoo of a butt?"

"A butt?" Malcolm squealed, examining the tattoo. "That's my wife! Well, she's in there somewhere." He moved the skin and wrinkles on his shoulder around, searching for her. "Nobody tells you that you're gonna get wrinkly shoulders when you get to my age. Ahh, forget it."

Charlie furrowed his brow and said, "You know, with all the technological advancement I've seen in my lifetime-"

"And that's long, you ol' fart," Malcolm said, laughing.

Charlie continued, "I'm disappointed nobody's invented a robot to scratch my butt."

Ben looked at me and smirked. When he had said that at our science fair presentation, I, along with everyone else, thought he was a bit of an idiot.

Malcolm was back studying his shoulder. "She did have kind of a butt face, but this is ridiculous."

"Malcolm, you turd."

"Ha ha, good one, Carl," Charlie said. "Turd. Such as great word. That's my one regret in life. I never called Malcolm a turd."

"Do it now!" Ethel yelled.

"Yes! Malcolm, you turd!"

"That's your only regret?" Sophie asked. "I would've thought that at your age, well, there might be a few more."

"Nah, that's pretty much it," Charlie said.

Carl asked, "Have you peed in Malcolm's slippers yet?"

"I do that once a week."

"Ooh, I've never done that," Ethel said.

"Why would I need a wood chipper?" Malcolm asked.

Carl looked at Charlie and said, "Did we have our farting contest today? I can't remember."

"I don't know. No reason we can't do it again."

"Why don't you do it after dinner?" Sophie suggested.

Carl let one rip.

"I guess not," Ben said, shaking his head.

"Good one, Carl!" Charlie yelled. In fairness, most of the people at Vintage yelled.

"I'm outta here," Ethel said, shaking her head.

Malcolm looked around and said, "Anybody hear a tug

boat horn? I coulda sworn I heard something. Reminded me of when I was in the Navy."

Charlie let one rip, even louder than Carl's. Even though he won, Charlie didn't look overly enthused.

"Can I get a diaper check?" Charlie asked me.

"Umm, I think you're good. It sounded dry," I said.

Sophie nearly threw up in her mouth.

"Ah, what would you know about wearing diapers? When was the last time you were in one, Alvin?

Sophie looked at me and laughed.

Charlie looked at me and said, "Your breath is terrible, Alvin! Oh, wait. I think that's me. I do need a diaper change. Wheel me inside."

I walked behind Charlie's wheelchair and started pushing him. I stopped and turned back to Sophie and Ben. "I don't know how long this'll take. Maybe meet me inside."

"Charlie!" Sophie yelled, as she jumped from her seat and ran past me.

I turned quickly, having no idea what was going on. Charlie was rolling down the path without a pilot, bouncing along. Sophie was chasing after him, but losing distance. I started running, too, but had no shot at actually catching the runaway chair. I was just going to be there to pick up the pieces.

Charlie screamed, "Aaaaahhhhh!" all the way down the hill.

As we got down to the bottom of the small hill, Charlie's wheelchair started to slow down. The only problem? It was headed straight for a large pond and a gaggle of geese. Feathers, geese, and probably some geese poop flew everywhere, as Charlie's wheelchair hit a stone and stopped short, launching Charlie into the air. He soared over a few geese and belly flopped into the murky pond and disappeared beneath the surface.

Sophie approached the edge of the lake as Charlie stood up out of the water. I stopped at the edge next to Sophie as two workers waded into the water and helped Charlie ashore.

"Oh, my God! Charlie! I'm so sorry!" I yelled.

"What're you sorry for? That was the best thing that ever happened to me in the ten years I've been here. Let's do it again!"

20

I had a rat invasion to plan. For some reason, I trusted that Sal would deliver. I just needed to figure out how I would deliver them. On my way in to school, I saw Zorch sweeping the sidewalk. I caught his eye as I walked toward him. I didn't know what to say to him. He had helped me more than I could ever ask anyone to help. I think rats in his building would be where he drew the line. I needed info, but it would have to be a little sneaky.

"What's up, little buddy?"

"Hi," I said, stopping to talk to him.

"What's on your mind?"

"As you know, I'm a Zero."

"Don't say that," Zorch said, leaning on his broom.

"I don't mean it in a bad way. I'm not in Butt Hair's inner circle. They've taken over the teachers' lounge."

"Don't I know it. The teachers are going crazy."

"Not that I want to be in Butt Hair's cool kids' group, but I am a little jealous. I want to see what it's like in there. I mean, do they have a lot of windows? How's the ventilation?"

Zorch looked at me funny. "It's fine. Normal, I guess."

"I like architecture, so just curious. Any secret passageways?"

"Nah, we closed them all up. Teachers were escaping."

"Really?"

"No. What are you up to?"

"Nothing, I swear!" I felt bad lying, but he wouldn't understand this one. "My brother gets to go in there and I don't, and he won't tell me anything about it. He's a jerk like that." And a lot of other ways.

"Alright, get to class," Zorch said, as he went back to sweeping.

"See you later," I said with a wave.

I hustled inside and caught up to Luke and Just Charles as they headed down the hallway to our Advisory wing.

"Hey, guys," I said. "What's up?"

Luke said "I was just asking him how many points I get for putting Vaseline on the main office door handle?"

I said, "I'll give you ten."

"I want twenty."

I shrugged. "Okay. Twenty." I was making it up as I went along. "And, if Buthaire falls on his Butt Hair, I'll give you another hundred."

"Deal. Let's meet up after first period and head past the main office. Or if you get called down by the Speaker of Doom, we'll just meet you there."

"Can't wait," I said, following Just Charles into the classroom.

Surprisingly, the Speaker of Doom did not summon me, so we headed over to the main office together. I stopped a good fifty feet away with Just Charles and huddled near a large herd of sixth graders. At least they were good for something. Sixth graders still lacked confidence, so they used the nerd defense we used during gym. Huddle together and hope you're close to the middle. Their packs would thin out as the year went by, but it was still early enough in the year that we could use them to our advantage.

Luke walked toward the main office door and looked around, his eyes darting in every direction. I didn't see any teachers anywhere. He squeezed a tube of Vaseline onto the door handle and spread it around. He vanished into a moving herd of sixth graders and jumped out as he reached us.

It was perfect timing. Ms. Pierre walked up to the door, studying the files in her arms and then grabbed the door. It slipped from her grasp as she pulled and she fell flat on her back, files and papers were flying everywhere. As if that was not crazy enough, she put her hands on the floor behind her head and kicked up. She landed on her feet in heels like a ninja. I was impressed, but even more stunned. And possibly in trouble. She looked over at us as we stared at her. We quickly scattered like hamsters.

"Did you see that?" I asked as we turned the corner. "That was straight out of the movies, like Kung Fu Panda or something."

"That was incredible," Just Charles said.

"We should be afraid," Luke said. "Very afraid. She's Buthaire on steroids."

I didn't get summoned to the main office, so I was hoping that Ms. Pierre didn't know it was me down the hall. There were a lot of kids and we were all staring at her.

∿

WE SAT IN THE CAFETERIA, waiting for Ben to arrive. He was

almost never late. I hoped he hadn't gotten caught by any of our enemies.

"I'm starting to get worried," I said. "Ben didn't tell me he wasn't coming to lunch today."

Sammie said, "He had a surprise mission he was working on."

"He didn't tell me anything," I said.

"Do you think he got caught?"

Before Sammie could answer, Ben walked into the cafeteria all smiles. He hurried over to us.

"Dude," I said. "You're running missions without me?"

"Just a quick, fun one. I put 'Out of Order' signs all over the place."

"Like where?" Sophie asked.

"The vending machines, gym door, Randy's locker. It was fun."

"Twenty points, Benjamin," I said. "Good work."

"This is so much fun," Ben said, giddy. "How many points if I hit Randy with spitballs?"

"Fifty," I said, "But he might kick your butt. I'll give you a hundred if you hit him with spitballs and make him think Derek did it."

"I'll plan it out."

"What do we get with all these points?" Ben asked.

"I don't know," I said.

"Are we calling them points?" Sophie asked. "How about Freedom Funds or Davenpoints? Davendollars?"

Just Charles said, "I heard with Butt Bucks you can get a pony."

"When have you ever wanted a pony?" I asked.

"Never. But I like knowing that with hard work and frugal spending, one day I could buy a pony."

"I will work out some corporate sponsorships, okay? I'll talk to Max Mulvihill."

"Who's Max Mulvihill?"

I looked at Ben and then back at Just Charles. "Just a business-savvy friend. And you've inspired me. Let's take this up a notch."

21

At lunch, I saw the perfect opportunity to take it up a notch. There were few events in middle school that could create more mayhem than an old-fashioned food fight. And it just so happened to be meatballs marinara day.

As I walked back to my seat from the hot lunch line, I almost walked into Bobby Newman, one of Derek's friends on the baseball team.

"Whoa, dude," Bobby said. "I almost wore your meatballs."

"Sorry, man. That would've been messy." I was about go on my way, but a thought occurred to me. "Hey Bobby, do you still pitch for the baseball team?"

"Yep."

"Really? I heard the track kids saying they didn't think you would make the team this year."

"Oh yeah?"

"You should prove 'em wrong and hit Griffin over there with a meatball."

"Griff Dog? I can't do that to him."

"What about Insta Graham?"

"Yeah, I could do that to him."

"Fire when ready, dude," I said, heading back to my table.

I took a minor detour and walked behind a few kids from the track team eating lunch, including Griff Dog and Insta Graham. Most of them were on the Hero board and friends with the Peer Review Committee, getting special privileges. I knew a few of them from grade school.

I said, "Hey guys." I got a few grunts and nods. "Be on the lookout. The baseball team said you guys were so slow they were going to use you as target practice with the meatballs marinara."

"Oh, really?" Griffin said. "Let them try. We've got the best shot putter in the county and an All-American javelin thrower right here. We'll light them up."

"I'm not trying to start a war. I just wanted to warn you guys. See you, later."

"Thanks, Davenport. You're not as big of an idiot as your brother and Warblemacher say you are."

"Thanks, I guess," I said.

I hurried back to my table and slipped into the seat. I told the rest of my crew. "I think I just instigated a food fight between the baseball and track teams. Eat fast."

"What?" Sophie said.

"The opportunity presented itself," I said, stuffing my face with meatballs.

Ben pointed to the meatball that was soaring through the air from the saucy hand of Bobby Newman. Five or six other kids at his table, most of them on the baseball team, hurled their own meatballs. They arced across the sky like a medieval archer attack.

Griff Dog and Insta Graham looked up at the incoming

attack, but were too late to defend against it. The meatballs rained down upon the unsuspecting track team, rancid beef blasting in all directions, sauce splattering far and wide.

The track team responded quickly. Kevin Flanagan shot putted a meatball across the cafeteria, while Insta Graham went full on wacko and used his whole tray like a discus. It spun through the air like a square frisbee. The baseball team ducked under the table as it landed, delivering six devastatingly disgusting meatballs in one attack. The meatballs took flight from the impact and connected with the noggins of at least three baseball players' heads.

The sauce splattered across the girls' softball team's table. Before we knew it, they were rifling meatballs underhand at nearly ninety miles an hour, taking out anyone and everyone who even dared to move in the cafeteria.

As awesome as Meatball Mayhem was, it was only a matter of time before I was caught in the crosshairs. And after the beef stroganoff blast that I took to the face from Derek on the first day of sixth grade, I wanted no part of being on the receiving end of a moldy meatball.

"Let's get out of here!" I yelled.

"Stay low!" Ben yelled.

We ducked, dodged, and rolled our way to the exit doors. There were ten wide open feet from the last table to the doors. We ran as fast as we could to freedom. I screamed as it rained meatballs all around us. Sophie was first to the doors. She hit them at full speed, blasting them open. The rest of us followed quickly and forced the doors shut. The sound of splattering meatballs echoed through the doors.

"That was close," I said.

Mr. Muscalini was standing right behind us, a confused look on his face.

"What's the matter, Mr. Muscalini?" Sophie asked. "You missed lunch."

"Davenport, does your nerd knowledge extend to cars?"

"Not really. What's wrong?"

"Someone put an out of order sign on my car."

"So?" I said. "Isn't it your car?"

"Yeah," Mr. Muscalini answered, scratching his head.

"So how would they know?" I asked.

"They wouldn't. Thanks, Davenport. I almost squashed it with a Hulk hammer fist. You really helped me out of a jam. I won't forget this."

"I'd particularly appreciate it if you remembered it the next time you want me to play dodgeball."

"You know I can't do that. The life skills are too plentiful."

There was a pounding on the door behind us. I wasn't sure if it was more meatballs or a person.

"Don't open it!" Ben yelled.

"Take cover!" I said, opening the door.

I opened it a crack, but no one was there. I looked down to see a saucy hand reaching toward me. "Help Mrs. Funderbunk, please," Mrs. Funderbunk said, weakly.

I grabbed her saucy hand and pulled. Sophie joined in. Once we got her through the door, Mr. Muscalini slammed the doors shut with a grunt, more meatballs pummeling the door.

Mrs. Funderbunk was in bad shape. Her white blouse was splattered from top to bottom with sauce. Her glasses were crooked and one lens was cracked. Her normally beautiful hair was full of meatball chunks.

"It's a war zone in there," she said.

Mr. Muscalini looked at her and asked, "Any good arms for my baseball team?"

$\sim$

A PERIOD LATER, I walked with Sophie on my way to class when Just Charles ran up to us.

"I'm so glad I found you. Sal and Luke are loading up the rats as we speak."

"What? How? We never even came up with a plan."

"He made one up, I guess. They're going to be released right after Randy and Regan start their lunch in the teachers' lounge."

I looked at Sophie and shrugged. "Sounds like a pretty good plan."

"The rats are locked and loaded," Just Charles said. "There were a lot of them, though. How many did you ask for?"

"I don't know. I said a couple. A couple is two, right?"

"You told me you said, a few," Sophie said.

"Maybe. A few is three. Well, three isn't a lot, right?"

"Yeah, there weren't three," Just Charles said, with a concerned look on his face.

"Well, how many are there?" I asked.

"A few more."

"Like how many?" I asked.

"Oh, twenty or so."

"Aah, farts. Zorch is gonna be so angry."

"Well, he won't know it's us, right?" Sophie asked.

"I kinda asked him about all the windows, vents, and secret passages in the teachers' lounge. I figured with two or three rats, it wasn't going to be an issue."

"This is going to be an issue," Sophie said.

22

I sat in English class, wondering what was going to happen with the rats. It was certainly going to be mayhem. And while earlier I thought that there wasn't much anyone could do to top a food fight, twenty rats in the teachers' lounge was quite possibly one of those events.

The door was open and I hadn't heard anything go down. The teachers' lounge was down at the end of our hallway. Mrs. Conklin was plowing through her lesson as always. My mind wandered, wondering if she was related to Calvin Conklin, the news anchor. I had never made the connection before.

I was jolted from my day dreaming by screams. Loud, shrieking screams. And then pounding footsteps with even more high-pitched screams. It was happening. The footsteps grew louder. I stared at the doorway, waiting to see what was happening. Randy sprinted by, his arms flailing above his head. Apparently, it was his shrieking we had heard. Regan followed quickly with the rest of the Peer Review Committee.

Even louder, shriekier screams headed toward us with

heavier, pounding footsteps. And then Mr. Muscalini sprinted by, high stepping as a dozen rats kept pace with him. A few students from my class ran to the door, trying to figure out what was going on, as if it wasn't obvious. I mean, I know that I had the inside track, having set the whole thing up, but there were people running with rats chasing them. What else was there to know?

They quickly figured it out, though, as five or six rats rushed into our classroom. Kids scattered among even louder shrieks. I hopped up onto my chair as did most other kids in my class. I looked around the room, admiring the mayhem, and chuckling to myself as Mrs. Conklin continued talking about Shakespeare, unaware that anything was going on.

One rat tore into Robyn Fletcher's bag and started gnawing through a granola bar. I didn't know rats liked fiber. She screamed and swatted at it with her folder, while Bryce Simon swung from the chandelier. I told you, my middle school was nice.

Zorch zoomed down the hallway, keys jiggling and chasing rats with a broom. "Outta my house, filth!"

It eventually settled down after all the rats disappeared. The class was a little disappointed when Mrs. Conklin announced a quiz for the following day based on that day's information. Information that none of us had heard.

But it was worth it when I saw Principal Buthaire later that day ,and it looked like he had lost half his hair since the last time I saw him. His eyes were bloodshot and he was running around frantically. So much so that he didn't even see me, let alone accost me with a detention.

~

WE MET up at Frank's Pizza after school to regroup and plan out our next item of mayhem. It was just the boys. Sammie had cheerleading practice and Sophie had to go somewhere with her mom.

I took a swig of my drink. "That went pretty well, don't you think?" I said, not sure at all.

"What's next?" Ben asked.

"We're going to hit them where it hurts the most."

"You're gonna kick Prince Butt Hair in the crotch?" Luke asked.

Just Charles added, "You'll definitely get detention for that."

"It would be worth it, but, no, that's not what I was talking about. But ten thousand points, or whatever it is we decide, for anyone who accomplishes that."

"Will that get me a pony?" Just Charles asked.

"I'm still working out the kinks, but probably not." I wanted to shut down any more conversations about ponies. I looked at Luke. "Maybe you can talk to Sal about that one. Or maybe Amanda Gluskin would do it."

"No way, dude. Sal asks me every day on the bus to come over and see the skin his snake just shed. He saves it. How gross is that?"

"Like wearing fur underwear in the summer?" I asked.

"It was a fur coat, not underwear."

"We all know you had a matching pair of underwear. But moving on, there's no crotch kicking. We're keeping it in the rodent family."

"Are you sure about this?" Ben asked.

"Yes."

Luke asked, "Where the heck are we gonna get more rats? Sal said he spent like a hundred bucks for those."

"Well, we can't pay him back, but give him like five hundred points for that. Tell him, he's leading the league. But we won't be needing any rodents."

"I'm confused," Just Charles said.

"Well, instead of releasing them, we'll be stealing one very important rodent."

"No! You can't steal Grimmwolf the Gopher!" Ben yelled.

"Shhh. I can. And I will. How many Davenpoints do I get for that?"

"A thousand," Ben said.

Just Charles said, "I hate to burst your bubble, but it's homecoming next Saturday. They'll be on high alert. It's an impossible mission."

"Yeah," Luke said. "The Riverside Rumble Ponies have been trying for thirty years, since my dad played football here for the Gophers. And they've never done it."

"They're not us. We're pulling an inside job," I said.

23

I wanted to spend the night planning the great gopher heist, but I had some volunteer hours to get in at Vintage. I sat with Ben, Carl, Charlie, and Malcolm. They were planning a crime of their own.

We were playing hearts, as they discussed the plan.

Carl leaned in and whispered, "Here's what we're gonna do, fellas. Now that we have Alvin and his fresh pair of eyes, he's our get-away driver. I nicked Phil's keys again. We're goin' to Vegas, Charlie!"

Malcolm threw down a card and said, "You're gonna die in the desert and be eaten by buzzards. Wait, do buzzards eat other buzzards?"

They ignored Malcolm.

Charlie looked at me and asked, "Can you see over the steering wheel? How did you even get your license?"

"I don't have it."

Charlie shrugged and said, "I can't hear a word you're saying, so just write it down some time. I probably can't read it, either. Oh, well. Where are my glasses?" They were right on top of his head.

"So, let's go," Carl said. "How much cash do you got?"

"Nothing," I said.

"What about you, Bert?"

Ben shook his head and said, "I got five bucks."

Charlie said, "That's kind of a problem. Carl's got twelve bucks in his butt."

I looked at Carl and said, "Why do you have money in your butt?"

"It's the only place to keep cash safe from the cleaning lady. But it's been in there for ten years. So, you're gonna take that out. You're much more nimble than I am."

"Are you sure it's still in there?" I asked. I looked at Ben and said, "You should probably check to see if it disintegrated."

"Yeah, right. I wouldn't do that for ten million, let alone ten bucks."

Carl said, "Malcolm, you coming with us?"

"I'm too old to break out of here. Plus, I don't want to miss my own birthday party."

"How old are you again?" Charlie asked.

"I think I'm gonna be ninety. Or eighty-five. Or a hundred."

"That's old," Ben said.

"You boys coming to my party?" Malcolm asked.

"I didn't know we were invited." I didn't really want to go, but I didn't know how to get out of it. "I'd have to check when it is and see if I'm on the schedule."

"Oh," Malcolm said.

~

I MADE it home for dinner. I needed to do some research on Grimmwald, the legendary gopher. I walked in the door with my dad as my mom was serving dinner. It was just the four of us. Leighton was out at a friend's house, studying. Derek had just gotten home from practice, so I had to endure his idiotic butt chin and behavior.

As I cut my chicken, I said, "Big game next week, huh?"

"Since when do you care?" Derek asked, rudely, of course.

"Since Dad started teaching me. The 44 Blast got me out of a big jam at the Medieval Renaissance fair."

My dad's face lit up. "It is a big game. We've been playing the Rumble Ponies during homecoming since I was a kid. They always tried to steal Grimmwolf, but never could. Clowns." Dad shook his head.

"How is Grimmwolf protected?" I asked.

"It's pretty elaborate, from what I hear. Some of the boosters talk about it," my dad said.

"What? Like biometric eye scanners and passwords inside of briefcases that are handcuffed to Mr. Muscalini?" I asked.

"No, that would be ridiculous. It's just your basic lasers, body doubles, fake media schedules, voice-enabled security systems."

"Grimmwolf has a media schedule?" Derek asked, shocked.

"Yes, Calvin Conklin from Channel 2 News interviews him every year."

"Really? What does he say?" Derek asked.

"Mr. Muscalini pretends to talk for him. He does a pretty good impression."

It was pretty ridiculous, but there was a lot more wrong there than a gopher's media schedule. I asked, "That's what interests you? Our school is using body doubles and lasers to protect a gopher and you want to know about the gopher's interviews? I guess that is pretty interesting, but still." I shook my head. It was going to be harder than I thought.

"It's pretty funny, actually," my dad said. "He uses a really deep voice and trashes the Rumble Ponies. I think it psyches them out."

I was kinda psyched out myself. I didn't know how in the world I was going to manage this heist when lasers and body doubles were involved.

⌒

BASED on the intel I had gathered at dinner about Grimmwald the Gopher's security detail, I called an emergency team meeting. I met the crew at the library after dinner. We had a cool tween/teen section that basically nobody used.

We sat around a large, circular table. Everyone from the crew was there, except for Sammie. She was bogged down with homework after cheerleading practice. Sophie, Ben, Luke, Just Charles, and Cheryl Van Snoogle-Something sat in a circle around me.

Ben called the meeting to order. He didn't have any Parmesan cheese, because that would be weird, so he just slapped his palm on the table. "Welcome to the Operation: Homecoming Heist planning session. I will let our mission leader take it from here."

"Thank you, Benjamin," I said. "I wrote out a list of things we need." I scrolled through my iPad notes. "We need mirrors, mountain climbing ropes, night vision goggles, and schematics of the locker room and Mr. Muscalini's office. Oh, and a recording of Mr. Muscalini saying the password."

"That's a tall order,' Sophie said.

"Oh, and a hot dog," I added.

"Make that two hot dogs," Luke said.

"What do you need a hot dog for?" I asked.

"I'm hungry," Luke said.

"I'm not using mine to eat."

"Order another one if you're hungry. Why do you care what I do with my hot dog?" Luke asked, annoyed.

"Because I'm trying to plan the greatest heist that Cherry Avenue has ever seen and you're slowing us down because you're hungry."

"I'm not hungry now. I'm just preparing in case I'm hungry during the heist."

"Moving on." I looked at Just Charles. It was going to be the hardest ask of anyone. "I need Wood Charles."

Just Charles' face dropped. "My stuffed Woodchuck?" His voice peaked two octaves higher. He then looked at Cheryl and said with his deepest voice, "Yeah, of course. If I still have it. I mean, I probably burned it in a bon fire. It's what men do. We burn kids' stuff in fires."

"That sounds really mean," Cheryl said.

"Well, it was my kid stuff." He turned back to me. "I'll see what I can do."

"Anybody have a cat?" I asked.

Cheryl said, "I do." She looked concerned.

"Don't worry. Your cat will be fine. Just Charles isn't going to burn him at the stake or anything. We just need a travel case or something to put Grimmwolf in once we capture him. By the way, I deserve more than a thousand points for pulling this off. My dad said Riverside has tried for thirty years with no luck."

Even I was buying into the whole points thing and I was making them up out of thin air.

"Any word on the corporate deals for the Davenpoints?" Just Charles asked.

"Yeah, huge progress. We're fine tuning some stuff with Burger Boys." Everyone looked less than impressed. I added, "and SpaceX," I said.

"What's that?" Luke asked.

"The dude who runs Tesla is going to send people up into space."

"Dude, that's what I'm saving my Davenpoints for!" Just Charles said.

"Me, too," Luke added.

I didn't want to tell them it would cost 200 million Davenpoints.

We totally need code names," Luke said. "I want to be Ghost Walker."

"Let's worry about the essentials first." At least it was better than when he wanted to name our band Lit Fart.

"My uncle has rock climbing stuff. I'll try to get some ropes," Sophie said.

"I'll get the hot dogs," Just Charles said. "Do you want ketchup on yours?"

"I prefer mustard," I said, without thinking. "I don't need any condiments. It's to test the lasers."

"We can get a bunch of those pocket mirrors at CVS," Cheryl said.

"Okay, and we probably need double-sided tape for those, too," I added.

"Consider it done," Sophie said. "How about a flashlight instead of the night vision goggles?"

"Do you want this mission to fail?" I asked.

"Of course not."

"Then we need the night vision. This is why Riverside has failed every year for the last thirty. Lack of commitment and resources."

"Do you really think Mr. Muscalini has lasers protecting a gopher?" Ben asked.

"He thinks dodgeball teaches us life skills, so anything is possible," I said.

24

I knew that Zorch wouldn't be down with stealing the gopher. He was a big football fan. I think he actually played for the team back in the day. He was kind of old- forty-two. I wasn't sure if they even played football back then. But then I realized he was pretty much the same age as my dad, so I guess they did.

As soon as the bell rang after eighth period, I rushed to Zorch's lair. He was usually there until the buses left. I slipped in and said, "Hello?"

"Hey, buddy. How's it going?"

"Good. Just checking in."

"Sit," he said. "Just move those papers."

I picked up the papers and sat in the chair. I looked at the blueprints in my lap and scanned them. "These are so cool. How do you actually read them?" I asked.

"It's not that difficult if you know the scale and the grid." Zorch leaned forward and pointed to them both.

I was busy analyzing the gym, locker room, and Mr. Muscalini's office for key entry points. I took a snapshot with my mind, hoping it would stick.

"Nice," I said, "Thanks. What's the deal with the rats?"

"Got rid of 'em. I have no idea how they got in here."

Before he could ask me if it was me, I said, "I wanted to tell you that even though there was a video of the Goat Turd performance, I couldn't see the wire, so I think we're clear there."

"That's good to know. Thanks."

"Thanks for the help. I have to catch a teacher before he leaves. See you tomorrow."

"See ya, buddy. Have a great rest of the day."

The jury was still out on whether or not that would happen. It all depended on our next task.

After that, the plan was to head to the gym. I met up with Ben. We were going to try to get Mr. Muscalini to say the password without realizing it, so we could use the recording to get into Grimmwolf's habitat. We walked against traffic toward the gym.

How are we gonna get the password?" Ben asked.

"It's probably about his biceps or something. It could be 44 Blast, though."

"Dodgeball is life. Make sure you get him to say it, like 'Dodgeball is life, Davenport!'"

"If there's no blood, get up and get it done! What's that other thing he says all the time, 'Sky's out, bis and thighs out?'"

"Suck it up, Gordo."

"You've brought shame to your whole family, Davenport."

As we entered the gym, Mr. Muscalini was leaving the locker room en route to football practice. He stopped when he saw us.

"I'm surprised to see you in the gym when you're not forced to be here."

"Well," I said. "We wanted to talk to you. You may know that our close, personal friend, Cheryl Van-Snoogle Something is a rising star, writing for the Gopher Gazette."

"Yes, I know of Ms. Van Snoogle-Something's journalistic talent."

"Well, she's very busy of course with the next article, but she wanted to do a piece on you. We told her how inspirational you are," I said, laying it on thick.

"Oh, why thank you, gents. I'm never sure if I'm getting through to you guys, particularly you nerds."

"We'd like to call it, Mr. Muscalini's Words of Wisdom," Ben said. "We were hoping you could just yell 'em all out, preferably at us." Ben pushed his pocket unnaturally toward Mr. Muscalini. He was too busy wiping tears from his eyes to notice.

"When I was a little boy, I dreamed of being a motivational speaker. Of writing a book. Motivations by the Mus."

"This could be the start of it!" Ben yelled.

I kind of felt bad. But not bad enough. We were still going to steal the Gopher.

"Let's see. If there's no blood, get up and get it done. What else? Even if there's blood, it can still be fun."

"What about if you needed to motivate a particular person, a nerd for example?" I asked.

"Sometimes kids need tough love. Suck it up. That usually works. It's my go to."

"Say it to me!" Ben yelled.

"Suck it up, Gordo!"

Ben followed, "Anything about the great game of dodgeball?"

"I can go on for hours. Dodgeball is life. It teaches resilience, teamwork, and important physical skills like strength and agility."

"What about the lifestyle quotes you always say? Mainly about your biceps and thighs," I said.

"Oh, yeah. They're life changing for people. Let's see. There's sun's out, guns out. Skies out, thighs out, or Skies out, bis out. Or both. Sun's out, buns out, but that's only in the privacy of your own home."

Ben looked at me. I nodded. We had what we needed.

"That was truly inspiring, Mr. Muscalini," I said.

Ben added, "I've never been that into sports, but you make me want to play some."

"Stick to rock, paper, scissor, gentlemen. But you'll be awesome at it! I hear it's going to be in the next Olympics."

25

———

The snapshot I took of the blueprints in my mind worked. Our heist crew of Ben, Luke, Just Charles, and I gained entrance to the ceiling above the boys' locker room and Mr. Muscalini's office via an HVAC utility closet that had a ladder leading up to a crawl space.

Since it was my mission, I was going into the office and taking Grimmwolf. The rest of the crew were there to support me. The boys all had backpacks holding all of our equipment. I was sitting on a beam just above Mr. Muscalini's office with the crew behind me. I had a harness around my waist, secured by the rock-climbing ropes that Sophie had provided. I would've felt more comfortable had she been there, but we felt it was best to keep her out of the boys' locker room. We got lucky I didn't get caught during my journey into the girls' locker room.

"Where's the night vision?" I asked. "Seriously, I want 500 more Davenpoints if I'm doing it without the night vision." Even I was buying into my own fake Davenpoints currency.

"The lights are on," Ben said.

"Still, it's so much cooler with the night vision."

I looked down through the ceiling into a sea of red lasers zig zagging across Mr. Muscalini's office. Through it, I could see the metal cage of Grimmwolf the Gopher, his terrifying teeth literally gnawing at the metal. It was time for step one. Avoid peeing in my pants. Step two was to assess the lasers. Were they trip wires or slice-you-in-half kind of lasers? I wasn't sure how to tell. I could've checked YouTube, but I was pretty certain that my cell service wasn't going to be all that good in the ceiling of the concrete locker room. I probably should've prepped a little more for the mission. My parents would probably be mad if I died trying to steal a dumb gopher.

"There are mirrors everywhere," I said. The lasers seemed to bounce from one mirror to the other.

Just Charles whispered, "Probably to check out his biceps from every angle."

"Hotdog," I said, like a surgeon asking for a scalpel in the operating room while holding my hand out. Mirror. STAT."

Just Charles slapped a cold, wet hotdog in my hand while Luke handed me a mirror. Would it have killed Just Charles to give me a hotdog in a ziploc or something? I decided to go for the mirror. I reached down through the hole in the ceiling with the mirror, looking to cut off the laser and isolate the beam and a whole bunch of other technical nerd stuff that I won't bore you with. Because the stupid hot dog hadn't been secured in any type of protective and non-slippery container, it rolled across the ceiling and fell down through the hole.

I reached for the hot dog as it fell, my voice letting out a slow-motion, "Nooooooo."

The hot dog sliced through the laser beam and hit the top of Grimmwolf's cage. It bounced and then settled halfway into his cage. Grimmwolf nibbled on it with great pleasure. No alarms went off. No hot dogs were sliced in half. I grabbed the cat bag that had Wood Charles inside and said, "Lower me down." Just Charles' incompetence saved us a ton of time and we were gonna need it. Mr. Muscalini was coming, although I didn't know it yet.

The guys lowered me down with the rope secured around my waist. I hung above the floor, not wanting to touch it for fear of leaving footprints or any other evidence behind. I stared at the lock that sat atop Grimmwolf's cage. My gloved hand reached into my pocket to remove my phone.

And then I realized that I made a huge mistake. I couldn't use my phone with my gloves on. It was going to slow me down. I put the phone back in my pocket, removed one glove, and then tried again. I punched the password into my ungloved hand and hit my recording app.

Mr. Muscalini's voice repeated the phrases we had gotten him to say during our fake interview. "If there's no blood, get up and get it done. Even if there's blood, it can still be fun."

Nothing happened. The lock was still perfectly secure. Grimmwolf stared me down like he was going to eat me. Thankfully, the thing was only a few pounds.

The recording continued, "Suck it up, Gordo. Dodgeball is life. Sun's out, guns out."

Nothing happened. I was starting to lose hope.

"Sky's out, thighs out, or sky's out, bis out. Sun's out, buns out."

The lock purred and clicked open. "We got it," I whispered and almost started cracking up. I'm glad he told us that one.

I removed the lock, opened the cage door, and reached my glove hand into the cage. Grimmwolf sprung like a coiled rattlesnake. The vicious gopher sunk its oversized teeth (that it had clearly been sharpening on the metal cage) into my thumb.

"Owww," I said, a little louder than I liked.

Grimmwolf continued to tug on the finger of my glove, thrashing about. It did have a lot of fight in it. And Mr. Muscalini obviously had him on a workout regimen. I wanted to put my other glove on, but I couldn't get Grimmwolf to let go of the first glove. I had to go in barehanded, which was a big risk for a beast such as Grimmwolf.

I quickly grabbed the hotdog that was still stuck in the top of the cage and plucked it out. Grimmwolf caught sight of it, let go of my glove, and snapped at the hotdog. I thrust it into his mouth and reached my hand around his body and picked him up. I could barely lift him with one hand. I threw Grimmwolf into the cat bag that was attached to my waist and grabbed Wood Charles. I threw the stuffed animal in the cage and zipped up the cat bag as Grimmwolf growled. He was a nasty bugger. I tugged on the rope just as a pair of keys jiggled outside of the office door.

"Pull me up!" I whispered.

"We're trying. We're nerds!"

26

The door creaked open just as my feet cleared the hole in the ceiling. I carefully slid the ceiling tile back in place as Mr. Muscalini entered.

Mr. Muscalini said, "Hey, buddy." After a quick pause again, he spoke, "I said, hey buddy!"

His voice bellowed, "What the heck is this? Grimmwolf!! Those Riverside punks finally did it. I can't believe they did it on my watch! I'm never gonna make the Gopher Hall of Fame. Not even with these biceps. Even they can't cheer me up. I smell inferior protein. Why does it smell like hot dogs in here? Has Zorch been in here again?"

Sophie was waiting for us outside, guarding our bikes.

"You got it?" Sophie asked, her eyes bulging.

"Why are you so surprised?"

"Because Riverside has tried for thirty years and they couldn't do it. Wow! Well, your chariots await."

"Did we really have to sacrifice Wood Charles for this?" Just Charles asked.

"No, but it's time to move on, buddy," I said.

We rode home on our bikes, Grimmwolf riding shotgun

in the basket on Sophie's bike. It was the best ride of my life. We had accomplished an impossible mission. A mission that our rival Rumble Ponies couldn't accomplish over the past thirty years.

~

SCHOOL MORALE WAS IN SHAMBLES. Not only was Principal Buthaire's Butt Bucks system weighing on so many of us, but news of our missing beloved (only to those who didn't really know him) mascot, Grimmwolf the Gopher, spread like wildfire.

By the end of the day, Cheryl Van Snoogle-Something had submitted a masterpiece of an article to the Gopher Gazette. She blamed it on Riverside, claiming that they finally got the better of us in the Homecoming prank.

The excitement didn't last for long. First off, I had no idea how to take care of a gopher, especially with Grimm-wolf's downright nasty demeanor and low-carb lifestyle. I wondered if the two were connected. I had him hidden in our shed. I found an old hamster cage in my basement and forced the beast inside of it. I went outside twice each night to check on him in the night and lost a glove each time in the process. When I checked on him in the morning before school, Grimmwolf was using them as bedding. There was no chance I was getting them back anytime soon as he snored atop them, his lip quivering with each exhale.

On top of that, Cheryl had another setback. As the Freedom Fighters gathered in the Atrium before school, Cheryl rushed over to us, visibly upset. Her eyes were barely holding in tears.

Just Charles asked, "What's the matter?"

"Ms. Pierre wouldn't publish the Grimmwolf article I

wrote. They don't want Riverside to know about it. They don't think Riverside did it."

"Why not?" I asked, nervously.

"Riverside would have it all over social media. So, they're actively investigating the kidnapping."

"They're calling it a kidnapping? It's a gopher," I said, rubbing my face with my hands.

"This isn't good," Sophie said.

"They're right, though," Ben said. "Calvin from the news would probably be all over this if Riverside had him."

"Yeah, Ms. Pierre said that he keeps calling Mr. Muscalini for his Homecoming interview. They called again for Mr. Muscalini when I was in the office," Cheryl said.

"So, what's next?" Luke asked.

I looked at Sophie, "I think you should pick the next one."

She thought for a moment. "Let's let the air out Prince Butt Hair's tires."

"I like it. Devastatingly effective. Minimal planning or tools. No hotdogs needed," I said.

Luke asked, "Who says hot dogs aren't needed? I'll take one."

"Who says you're even invited on this one?" I asked.

"Maybe I'll let the air out of his tires myself. How many Davenpoints do I get? By the way, how many points do I need to get to space?"

"Still working out the details. I'll know soon. And there's no reason you can't let the air out of Butt Hair's tires tomorrow or next week, after Sophie and I do it."

"Good point. Sign me up. I'm on a mission to Mars."

~

Sophie and I met up outside of school after the final bell. I had to hurry to get there in time so we could let the air out of Buthaire's tires and still make it onto our buses for a clean getaway.

We slipped through the line of buses and slinked through the packed parking lot. Teachers wouldn't be too far behind. Some of them hate school even more than we do. The bell rings and they're knocking kids out of the way to beat them out the door.

Principal Buthaire's car was some sort of Buick, charcoal in color. We just called it The Buttmobile. I assure you, it wasn't anywhere near as cool as the Batmobile. I'm sure Principal Butt Hair fantasized about having all of Batman's weapons and gadgets to catch me breaking all of his ridiculous rules, but all he had was heated seats. Gotta keep that butt hair warm.

He was usually one of the first to get to school, so we searched through the first few rows closest to the school and quickly found it.

"There's the Buttmobile," I said, pointing toward it.

Sophie laughed. "I didn't know you called it that."

"Yep. I'll hit the front tire while you hit the back. And then if we have time, we'll get the other side."

"Sounds like a plan," Sophie said, her eyes focusing on the tire as she approached it. She was in Sophie beast mode, which was still beautiful, but if you were her target, get ready to be destroyed.

I knelt down next to the front tire and looked around as I unscrewed the cap. I used my thumbnail to press on the pin. The air hissed out of the tire. It was one of the sweetest sounds I had ever heard. It was like a beautiful, Buthaire-crushing wind ensemble.

And then I heard something that was less than the sweetest sounds ever.

"Do you hear voices?" Sophie asked.

"Uh, oh. Get under the car." I rolled underneath the car on my stomach.

Sophie followed me underneath. I looked over at her.

"Hey," I said.

"Hey."

We looked out into the parking lot from underneath the car, only seeing whatever was straight back from the trunk of The Buttmobile, which happened to be Mr. Gifford's yellow punch buggy. A pair of shiny men's shoes walked behind the car. It was Principal Buthaire!

Principal Butt Hair was singing something. "Detention is my favorite invention. Don't be late or you won't graduate. Davenport, you're so short and you stink at sports..."

I looked at Sophie, eyes bulging. The car alarm chirped

from underneath the hood of the car we were under. The good news was the car wasn't going anywhere without any air in its tires and you can probably figure out the bad news.

I crawled out from underneath The Buttmobile and rolled like a log until I was underneath the car next to it. Sophie was right behind me. I scooted underneath to the other side and moved out of the way so Sophie could get out from underneath it. I crawled on my hands and knees to the front tire and squatted down while Sophie followed. Prince Butt Hair's car door slammed.

"Now, what it the heck is going on here?" He paused for a minute and then yelled, "Davenport!" For once, he was right.

But we weren't going to stick around to prove him right. Sophie and I crawled from car to car on our hands and knees, my butt in her face. I was glad that my body seemed to have handled the spicy beef and broccoli from lunch well. The last thing I needed right then was to fart in my girl-friend's face. That was an immediate break up as far as middle school was concerned.

Once we were far enough away, we stood up and ran to the buses. As Sophie was getting on hers, I asked, "How many Davenpoints do you want?"

"None, that was just fun, doing that with you," Sophie said, smiling.

Good. I was getting concerned at how many points I was promising everyone. I hustled to my bus and slipped into the seat next to Ben as the doors closed.

"Mission, complete," I said, smiling. "The Buttmobile has been defused."

27

The Speaker of Doom summoned me as expected. I sat in my personal chair, waiting for my interrogation from Principal Buthaire. Previously, I would've likely been a little nervous, but I had become numb to Butt Hair's bashings. As I nodded off in boredom, the main office door flew open, its hinges being stretched to its limits. Mr. Muscalini appeared in the door frame, barely fitting. He wiped his brow and walked toward me.

"Davenport, what are you doing here?"

I shrugged. "I don't know." I knew, but I had to pretend it was news to me. I was at least thankful he didn't think of me as the lowly degenerate that Butt Hair did.

Mrs.Murphy asked, "Mr. Muscalini, can I help you?"

"I need to see the principal," he said, agitated.

"What does it pertain to?"

"The kidnapping."

Mrs. Murphy rolled her eyes. "Ms. Pierre is taking the lead on that. You can go into her office."

"Thank you," Mr. Muscalini said, walking toward Ms. Pierre's open office.

He disappeared through the doors, but I could hear their conversation.

"Mr. Muscalini, what can I help you with?" Ms. Pierre said, curtly.

"I wanted to see Principal Buthaire about the kidnapping."

"Well, he's a very busy man. Is this about a gopher?" Ms. Pierre asked, seemingly holding back laughter.

"It's not just a gopher, it's our gopher. Grimmwolf- it's our secret weapon. It's the reason we fight like warriors," Mr. Muscalini said, his emotion rising with each word.

"We're doing everything we can."

"I want to cancel the game."

"You want to cancel Homecoming, a tradition for more than fifty years, for a gopher?"

"Postpone it then. We're gonna get killed."

Ms. Pierre answered calmly, "I'm not one for sports gatherings, but if my research is correct, we're the first-place team. They're terrible. The Riverside Rumble Ponies, is it? I mean, who can't beat a Rumble Pony? What the heck is a Rumble Pony anyway?"

"It doesn't matter! If we don't have Grimmwolf, we lose! This town is gonna go nuts. Mayhem will ensue! Mayhem has already been ensuing!"

As much as I wanted to continue listening to their conversation, Principal Buthaire called out to me, "Davenport! In here, now!"

I moped out of my chair and into The Butt Crack.

"Sit down, Misterrrrr Davenport," Principal Buthaire said firmly. "Somebody let the air out of my tires yesterday. Would you happen to know anything about that?"

"I don't know anything about cars, sir. I know a little bit about air. Maybe it wanted to be free?"

"Excuse me?"

"Maybe it was tired of being cooped up and wanted to get out of there."

Principal Buthaire didn't know how to respond, or at least that's what I surmised from the puzzled look on his face. I wondered if that should be my strategy going forward- just say ridiculous stuff to which he couldn't think of a comeback.

"I'm going to prove that you committed this heinous crime," Principal Buthaire said, pointing his finger at me.

"Is it a crime to let the air out of someone's tires? I mean, can you really say that you owned the air?"

"I paid to have the air put in the tires," he said, smiling.

"You paid for a service. Did you buy a particular amount of air?"

"No," he said, annoyed.

"I'm no expert, but I'm not sure what the crime is and I don't think that letting air out of the principal's tires in forbidden in the code of conduct."

"Not yet, it isn't," Principal Buthaire said, threateningly.

I didn't feel all that threatened by it.

～

LUNCH WAS EVEN MORE EXCITING, as the anger from the teachers started to bubble over. They were tired of having been displaced from their lounge, so Principal Buthaire could cater to the idiots enforcing his ridiculous code of conduct.

Mr. Gifford, Mr. Muscalini, and Mrs. Callahan sat down at the table next to us. Mrs. Funderbunk walked over, carrying her lunch tray, and sat down on the seat next to Mrs. Callahan. The seat, which was more like a wobbly saucer on a pole, teetered over. Mrs. Funderbunk crashed to the floor, dragging her food tray down with her. Mrs. Funderbunk wasn't my favorite teacher, but nobody deserves seafood surprise to the eyes.

Mr. Gifford scrambled to his feet to help Mrs. Funderbunk to her feet.

"Are you okay?" Mrs. Callahan asked.

Mrs. Funderbunk didn't say anything, as she dusted herself off. She straightened her blouse and finally spoke, "Mrs. Funderbunk will not stand for this!"

Mr. Muscalini cocked his head to the side and said, "You are standing."

"You know what Mrs. Funderbunk means," she said, annoyed.

"I do? I'm the Phys Ed teacher, not the psychic teacher."

"We don't have a psychic teacher."

"See? If I was the psychic teacher, I would've known that we had one."

Mr. Gifford chimed in, "Do you remember Miss Tabitha, the fortune teller from the Renaissance Fair? I might ask her out."

"What happened to your last girlfriend?" Mrs. Callahan asked. "I thought that was going well."

"My friend told her that I was Bill Nye, the Science Guy. When she figured it out that I wasn't, we broke up."

"Who wants to date Bill Nye, the Science Guy?" Mrs. Callahan asked.

"He's pretty high up in the science teacher food chain," Mr. Gifford said.

"This is about Mrs. Funderbunk and all educators. First the Meatball Mayhem and now this! We need to stand up for our rights!"

As interesting as the conversation was, our attention was

pulled toward a line of kids running out of the cafeteria. Three kids flew out of their seats, holding their stomachs, and sprinting toward the exit. And then two more on the other side of the room.

Sophie, Ben, and Sammie looked at me, expectantly.

"What?" I asked, defensively. "I don't know what's going on. Kids have been running out of here for the last year nearly every meal. It's probably the potatoes."

Everybody looked at me funny.

"The potatoes au gratin have gone rotten," I said.

28

Sophie and I volunteered at Vintage Retirement Community the night before the big Homecoming football game. I was hoping to hang out with some of the old ladies, but it was a no go. They all went to bed early. While the ladies could be a little annoying with all of the cheek pinching, none of them ever asked me to check or change their diapers, and they seemed to have a better handle on where their dentures were.

But, of course, I got stuck with Malcolm, Carl, and Charlie again. At least I was with Sophie. We played hearts again. I didn't dislike it, but they moved so slow, sometimes I'm not sure if they fell asleep while they're looking to pass some cards.

Sophie looked at Malcolm and asked, "Austin says you're having a big birthday party. What do you want?"

I stared at her, trying to signal to her to change the subject. I didn't want his birthday party coming up, because I didn't actually want to go to it. She didn't get the hint.

"Are you coming to my party, Alvin?" Malcolm asked.

"Not sure," I said. "I need to check with my parents."

"So, what do you want?" Sophie asked again.

"To get the heck out of this place for a day. Catch a football game or watch kids play in the park. Eat a steak."

"Can you do that with dentures?" Sophie asked.

"Nah, I can't do any of it. It's never gonna happen."

Carl looked at Charlie and said, "Instead of having a getaway driver, what do you think of that Uber thing?"

"Goobers? I used to love those."

"No. Uber."

"What's that?" Malcolm asked.

"Never mind," Carl said, shaking his head.

~

IT WAS SATURDAY MORNING. Homecoming. The big game was only hours away. I ate breakfast at the kitchen table with my dad. Derek was already at school, prepping for the big game. Mr. Muscalini wanted everyone super prepared, because he thought they were already at a huge disadvantage because of 'The Kidnapping.'

My dad threw on the TV while we ate and turned it to Channel 2 News. Calvin Conklin was front and center on the screen, an empty Gopher Stadium behind him.

Calvin held the microphone up to his mouth and said, "Channel 2 News reporting live. The normally gregarious and boastful head coach, former ping pong champion and Super Bowl triple backup kicker, Mr. "Mus" Muscalini, refused all interview requests for Grimmwolf the Gopher. Some are speculating that Grimmwolf has died. We have nothing other than hearsay at this point, but we're confident enough to be the first to call his death. Rest in peace, Grimmwolf. You will be missed."

A picture of Grimmwolf flashed on the screen, wearing a football helmet.

"What the-" my father said.

Calvin continued, "The Gophers were the clear-cut favorites heading into this game. The team is seven and one, and has beaten the Rumble Ponies every year for the past thirty. But the devastating loss of their beloved mascot has put all that in question. Cherry Avenue Middle School has not yet commented on the whereabouts of Grimmwolf, but it's clear. He's totally dead and this team might just get killed today. Back to you, Ted."

"That's totally ridiculous," my father said. "We're going to crush them."

I didn't really care, but I did appreciate the reminder from Calvin to feed the stupid gopher. I didn't want him to end up actually dead.

～

I SAT in the packed stands with Sophie and my parents. Despite the missing Grimmwolf, my dad was optimistic to start the game.

"We're gonna run Riverside over like we do every year."

"Even without Grimmwolf the Gopher?" I asked. "Mr. Muscalini was pretty upset about it. He wanted to cancel the game. He said we were gonna get crushed."

"That's a silly superstition, son. Our talent will win out."

The game started and it was pretty even. The Rumble Ponies looked energized, while The Gophers were seemingly just going through the motions.

"We look flat today," my dad said.

"Has this ever happened before?" I asked.

"Sometimes they start slow and then pick it up, but they look pretty bad today. They don't have that killer instinct."

"Hmm, that's interesting," I said, looking at Sophie.

The Rumble Ponies punted the ball deep into our territory, heading straight for Derek. He caught the ball on the fly and took off running off the field. The sleepy crowd started to buzz, as Derek zoomed in and out of traffic, missing tackles, spinning around defenders. He crossed midfield with only a few defenders in front of him. A small, but seemingly brave, Rumble Pony stepped up to attempt to stop Derek.

"Oh, Derek's gonna run him over," my dad said.

Derek lowered his shoulder and rammed the defender, knocking him down, but the defender's helmet had connected with the ball, knocking it from Derek's grip. The ball helicoptered through the air and then bounced onto the ground.

"No!"

The crowd groaned and rose to their feet as both teams wrestled for the ball in a huge pileup. It wasn't clear who had the ball.

"I think Nick got it. He was first to the ball. And good luck ripping it from his grip once he has it," my dad said, hopefully.

The refs cleaned up the pileup and pointed in the opposite direction from where The Gophers were going. The crowd groaned. A Rumble Pony held the ball above his head as the whole team celebrated. Derek stormed off the field and slammed his helmet onto the ground.

The Gophers' defense limited the Rumble Ponies to three plays and a punt. Derek caught the ball again, ran about twenty yards, and held onto the ball until he was forced out of bounds on the sideline.

"Okay, okay!" Dad yelled. "Here comes the 44 Blast! This is our chance!"

The Gophers' offense lined up with Randy at quarterback and Derek and Nick in the backfield. It was the formation they used to run the 44 Blast. I do pay attention from time to time.

The last time I had seen the Gophers run the 44 Blast, Derek made the Bisons look stupid. He ran into the end zone untouched and scored what proved to be the winning touchdown. The play was so good, it even worked for a nerd like me at the Medieval Renaissance fair. And the Rumble Ponies weren't the Bisons and they certainly weren't the Knights of the Undead, but that's a story for another time.

Randy's mouthpieced face yelled out a muffled, "My I.Q. is less than you. My I.Q. is forty two. Oh, and I'm totally snakelike!"

Randy faked the hand off to Nick and then gave it to Derek, who cut up the field, breaking a tackle to continue his run. A Riverside player burst out of a pack from nowhere, blasting Derek. I wish I knew how awesome that felt. My brother's legs flew out from underneath him and he landed flat on his back. The crowd groaned again.

"He's okay," my mom said.

My dad nodded his head and said, "Everybody makes a lucky play now and then. Nothing to worry about. Mr. Muscalini will call it again."

Randy stood behind center again and called for the ball, "Poo in my stew. Poo in my stew. I'm a cheater and very unsportsmanlike!"

The center snapped the ball to Randy. It was the 44 Blast again. He faked to Nick and handed it to Derek. This time a hoard of Rumble Ponies stampeded Nick and Derek, taking them both down in a heap and a cloud of dirt.

Once the dust settled, Derek got to his feet slowly, while Nick was a touch behind him. As soon as Nick's right foot hit the ground, he lifted it up and started hopping on his left foot. He hopped over to Derek and leaned on his shoulder. Derek and Mr. Muscalini helped Nick off the field. The Gopher crowd was dead silent. I was starting to think there was something to the whole Grimmwolf thing.

The game continued. Mr. Muscalini had lost his mind. He yelled at the refs. He yelled at the other coaches. He yelled at the Gophers. He yelled at himself. I think he may have even yelled at his mother. And none of it was motivational.

We got the ball back. The game was still tied. Nick was back in. We had a long way to go to score, but the Gopher crowd was optimistic. A ferocious, "Let's go, Gophers!" chant echoed throughout the stands.

"Okay, Gophers! Here we go!" my dad yelled.

Randy called out, "Farts! Farts! Whenever I bowl, I never get a strike!"

The center delivered the ball to Randy, who dropped back and surveyed the field. Randy looked left. Derek and Jayden were covered. He looked right. Nick had two guys on him. Randy scrambled, evading a pursuer, but ran out of room to run, and was sacked behind the line of scrimmage.

"What is going on?" my dad yelled, to no one in particular.

"Are they gonna go for it on fourth down?" my mother asked.

"No, they're gonna punt. There's still time left."

Kenny Messenger trotted out to the field and lined up for a long snap to punt. The center hiked the ball, which hit Kenny right in the hands, but he botched it. The crowd went silent. Kenny scrambled to pick up the ball. He grabbed it with two hands, as three defenders rushed toward him. Kenny took two quick steps and kicked the ball. Two of the defenders dove forward and stuffed the punt.

The ball bounced and then rolled. The third defender picked it up on the run and just kept going. He ran it all the way into the end zone for a touchdown. The Rumble Ponies went nuts.

And the rest of the game went pretty much like that. We lost 14-7 and it was all Grimmwolf the Gopher's fault.

As we walked out of the stadium, Calvin Conklin stood in front of the TV camera with a somber look on his face. "That stupid gopher killed the season. There's no hope for the Gophers to make the County Championship game with this historic loss. Frankly, Ted, I'm disgusted." He dropped the mic and walked off.

29

I kind of felt bad about the whole Grimmwolf thing. Mr. Muscalini was a mess and most of the football team was pretty depressed. True, a bunch of them were Peer Review Counselors, but I still didn't feel great about it. I decided to focus my efforts on something that wouldn't cause anyone an identity crisis or to question their life's purpose. Except Butt Hair. I wanted him to question his life purpose a whole lot, because he thought his was to ruin today's youth.

After Randy docked the debate club and the girls' volleyball team fifty Butt Bucks a kid for losing their respective matches, I knew it was time to escalate our battle against Butt Hair and his stupid system.

We had a virtual Freedom Fighters meeting online. All we needed was a Parmesan cheese shaker from Ben's house and access to the Internet. I sat at the desk in my bedroom, my iPad open in front of me. The app we used showed videos of each kid on the chat in little squares on my screen. It was the usual suspects: Ben, Sophie, Luke, Just Charles, Cheryl Van Snoogle-Something, and Sammie. Luke had invited Jasmine Jane to join us. I finally relented and let her in. I didn't want Luke to blame me when he got dumped. He had plenty of other faults that would eventually cause that.

Ben smacked the Parmesan cheese on his desk. "This meeting is now in session."

"I've been thinking," I said. "We need to take this up a notch."

"Are you serious?" Sammie asked.

"After everything we've done already?" Sophie asked, surprised.

"We need to support our debate team friends. They sank to Zero status after the loss to Bear Creek. Last I checked, the football team didn't lose any Butt Bucks for embarrassing the school in the lost to Riverside. The system is unfair."

"So, what do we do next?" Just Charles asked.

"I was thinking a walk out," I said, simply.

"I love a good old-fashioned walk out," Cheryl said.

"How many have you been a part of?" Jasmine asked.

"None, but my mom was involved in a lot of that kind of stuff when she was younger."

"Who would join us?" Sophie asked.

"Anybody who wants to," I said. "Students, teachers, the cafeteria staff, Zorch."

"How can we get the teachers involved?" Ben asked.

"What if we messaged them through the TeachMe app?" Just Charles asked.

"That's a great idea," I said. "We can hit the Freedom Forum and all the usual social media channels. As soon as the Speaker of Doom crackles, we all head out. We can send a message to Channel 2 News."

"I'll get working on the Forum," Cheryl said.

"Everybody hit up their teachers and then social media."

"Farewell, Freedom Fighters!" Luke yelled.

I disconnected the video feed and immediately messaged Mr. Gifford and Dr. Dinkledorf.

Dr. Dinkledorf responded to me in about six seconds. "I'll bring my bull horn!"

Mr. Gifford was just as excited. "Let's do this! Should we bring some duct tape and be done with this guy?" He was thinking of Principal Puma, who had been duct taped to the wall by the current tenth-grade class. My sister's class.

~

THE NEXT SCHOOL day started with a Peer Review Committee crusher. They met all of the unsuspecting students emerging from the buses with Butt Buck seizures.

I walked into the Atrium with Ben and Sammie. The Peer Review Committee was accosting kids left and right. Before I knew it, Randy was right in my face.

"Davenfart! What a glorious morning. I have something for you. Well, more like I'm going to take something from you."

"I gotta be somewhere, Randolph," I said, starting to walk away.

Randy grabbed my shoulder. "Wait just a minute. Let's make a deal."

I stopped and looked up at him. "And I should trust you to hold up your end of the deal?"

"Well, since we'd rather just hang out in the lounge than chase you around all day, we figured we'd just give you detention now, because it's easier for us." He held out a detention slip.

I stared at the detention slip and said, "And what's the other end of this great deal?"

"That's it. You take your detention now and I get to hang out in the lounge all day and not chase all of you idiots around all day."

"Stuff it up your butt, Randy. Things are about to change," I said, as I pushed his hand and the detention slip back at him and walked off. I rejoined Ben and Sammie and headed to Advisory.

I looked across the Atrium to see Principal Buthaire addressing at least eight security guards in red jackets. He stopped speaking and smirked at me. I didn't know what he was up to, but I didn't like it. I was glad, though, that he didn't give me detention.

As I turned the corner, I stopped abruptly. Ms. Pierre was standing in front of me.

"Misterrrr Davenport. I hear you are quite the busy bee, pollinating ideas. The thing about bees, though, is that they can only sting once, and then they die."

"That's really morbid," Ben said.

"It's science," she said.

"What is it with all of these insect analogies?" I asked under my breath.

"What's that, now?"

"Thanks for the lesson," I said. "Can I go now?"

"Yes. See you at detention." She handed me a detention slip with a smile.

I took it and threw out a sarcastic, "Thanks!"

I crumpled up the detention slip as I walked down the hall and launched it toward the garbage pail with a sky hook. Nick DeRozan swatted it to the ground. It was just like gym class.

I COULDN'T WAIT for the walk out. I just wanted to get out of that dump. I didn't care if anyone joined me or not. The good news was that it was only a few minutes away.

I walked into class and settled into my seat.

Just Charles nodded at me and asked, "Are you sure about this?"

"Absolutely," I lied.

The Speaker of Doom crackled. I looked around the room as a few students started to get up. Mrs. Callahan stood up and said, "I'm outta here. Let's blow this taco stand, people!"

And with that, everybody got up and headed for the doors. Just Charles held out his hand for a high five.

I just shook my head and said, "After, bro." I wasn't big on high fives. I just couldn't seem to get them right without risking broken bones.

Just Charles led the way into the halls. We were swept up into the madness, as swarms of kids headed for the exits.

"Are you seeing this?" Luke yelled to us.

"This is unbelievable!" I yelled.

I followed the crowd into the Atrium. I did a double take when I saw a bunch of red jackets scattered about.

Principal Buthaire stood up on a bench with a bullhorn and said, "Carmichael, detention! Flanagan, detention! Vanessa Becker, detention!"

Some kids started slinking back to class before they got too close to Buthaire.

"Where are you going?" I yelled to Jimmy Carmichael. "You already got detention. You might as well go outside."

Principal Buthaire and I locked eyes. He yelled into the bullhorn, "What have you done Mr Davenport? You're going to get expelled!"

I cupped my hands around my mouth and yelled back, "Your manual says that getting caught cutting school is two days of detention. How do Monday and Tuesday sound next week?"

His face burned red. I heard Ms. Pierre say, "He is a crafty one."

"This isn't finished, Misterrrr Davenport!"

"He's immune to detentions, sir. That means there's only one course of action left. Expulsion," Ms. Pierre.

Aaah, farts.

Before I knew it, a bunch of kids were turning back. I stood on my tippy toes and saw that the security guards were trying to block kids from leaving. I racked my brain trying to figure out what to do.

Dr. Dinkledorf beat me to it. He stood up on a table and yelled, "We must stand up in the face of tyranny! We shall not be ruled by an iron fist! Give me liberty or give me death!"

Somebody yelled, "I don't want to die for this!"

The rest of the school just stared at Dr. Dinkledorf. And then even more kids started walking back to class. I had to fight against them to keep going toward the exit.

Dr. Dinkledorf looked around and yelled, "Free pizza in the parking lot!"

Now, that was something everyone could get behind. Kids started screaming and rushing toward the doors. The thunderous footsteps shook the very foundation of the school.

It was the tide that turned the war. There was nothing like the promise of the spectacular combination of dough, cheese, and sauce baked to perfection from Frank's.

30

C alvin Conklin stood in front of the giant crowd facing the TV cameras. He smiled, revealing his pearly whites and said, "We got a tip from FreedomChick27 and it seems like one heck of a tip." He looked deep into the camera. "I've got a tip for you, too. If you run out of time because you've got a news tip to chase, but you're hungry and you haven't eaten breakfast, just put your toothpaste on your toast!"

Calvin paused with his hand on his earpiece and then looked back at the camera. "Ted says I need to talk about what's actually going on. Well, there is nothing short of mayhem here at Cherry Avenue Middle School amid a walkout supported by the teachers and students alike. It's probably just another bad batch of meatloaf. It's been voted the worst in the county four years running. It's barely newsworthy at this point." He looked at Mr. Gifford. "Anybody dead here?"

Mr. Gifford frowned and said, "No."

"Well, that's too bad. But it's a great opportunity for me to flash these pearly whites." He smiled into the camera. "I can't help but jump in front of the camera when the opportunity is there. You gotta seize the moment. Or the moment will sneeze on you. That's what my grandmother always used to say. In hindsight, I'm not sure why. She was a bit cuckoo, I know. Well, this has been fun. Calvin C. signing off. Back to you, Ted."

Calvin pressed his ear piece again and frowned. He looked back at the camera. "Well, Ted seems to think that was pretty poor coverage, so I'm actually gonna have to talk to some of these wackos."

Calvin looked at Mr. Muscalini and said, "Excuse me, sir. Do you want to tell the world why you're here?"

"No press, no photos!" Mr. Muscalini yelled, running away. "Without Grimmwolf, I don't know why I'm here. I have no purpose."

CALVIN HELD the microphone out to Mrs. Funderbunk. "Can you tell me why you've had a walk out?"

Mrs. Funderbunk looked into the camera. "Walkout? No! It's a celebration! Everyone is so excited for our upcoming musical! It's written and directed by the award-winning Madeline Funderbunk!"

"Is it the meatloaf?"

Mrs. Funderbunk smiled into the camera. "It's Funderbunk.com. Be sure to check us out. Hashtag: Broadway. Toodles."

Calvin looked into the camera, stars in his eyes. "That is some woman."

Dr. Dinkledorf walked over to Calvin and stood next to him. "I have something to say."

"Did you break out of Vintage Retirement Communities,

old man? My informant told me there was a huge escape in the works."

"I'm Dr. Mason Dinkledorf, the history teacher here. We are tired of being oppressed by the dictatorial regime of Principal Buthaire. The extent of this administration's corruption runs deep. We must drain the swamp."

Calvin looked like the old dudes at the VRC during hearts. I wasn't sure if he was still awake.

"We want equal rights," Dr. Dinkledorf said.

Someone in the crowd yelled, "We want free pizza on Fridays!"

Dr. Dinkledorf said, "No, we don't."

Calvin's eyes popped open. He asked, "Why not? That sounds pretty good."

"We want rules that make sense. We want the same rules to apply to everyone equally. The Principal seems to think he's a dictator and can enforce whatever he wants whenever he wants."

"Can't he? This is public school. I think that's how it works, no?"

Dr. Dinkledorf shook his head and walked off.

Calvin looked into the camera. "Let me talk to a student." He looked around and pointed at me. "You there! Are you FreedomChick27?"

"Umm, no," I said as he jammed the microphone into my face.

"You had to think about that for a second. Hiding your secret identity? What's your favorite number?"

"Eleven?" I said, not sure what was going on.

"Liar!" Calvin yelled. He held his hand to his earpiece. "Sorry, Ted." He looked back to me. "You look familiar."

Thankfully, I didn't have to answer that. Dr. Dinkledorf

returned with a bull horn, screaming into it, and scaring Calvin away.

Dr. Dinkledorf yelled, "Buthaire Bucks stink like butt!"

The crowd started chanting, "Duct tape him! Duct tape him!"

"Let's flip a car!"

"How about that yellow punch buggy!"

Mr. Gifford yelled, No!"

Thankfully, a bunch of pizza arrived, so nobody's car got flipped. After that, not a whole lot got done. People were too busy stuffing their faces to yell any chants and too embarrassed to eat near the cameras, so as to avoid getting caught on TV while eating like pigs. A lot of kids went back to school while the rest of us went to, you guessed it, Frank's, for more pizza. It was that good.

31

That afternoon, I had another volunteering session at the VRC and was set to get my paperwork signed for my credits for the semester. I hammered out a hard twenty hours of service to old people. It was hard work. I had no idea how people spent twenty years in prison. I nearly lost my marbles with ten sessions at two hours a pop.

I was saying my goodbyes to everyone, shaking hands, hoping Carl and Charlie didn't have a fart contest scheduled at that moment.

I felt a tap on my shoulder. I hoped it wasn't Ethel wanting to arm wrestle or anything. She was the only one I feared could take me down. She might even be able to slap me in a Camel Clutch.

I turned around. Thankfully, it was Jasmine Jane. "Hey, Jasmine. Didn't know you were here."

"I've got some hours to do here. It's not so bad. I play a lot of cards and watch Wheel of Fortune."

"Just stay away from Carl and Charlie around 12 P.M."

"Why is that?"

"You don't want to know. Just trust me on it."

"So, what's next on our agenda with the Freedom Fighters? I thought the walkout was better than expected. How are we going to create mayhem next?"

"Still working on it," I said, scratching my head. "The walkout was a big one. Not sure what else to do."

"You have no ideas?"

I had some ideas, but I wasn't ready to share them, especially with someone so new to the group. She wasn't in the inner circle.

"Nothing yet. We've been busy."

"Well, let me know when you figure something out. I'm happy to brainstorm."

"Thanks. My dad is waiting for me. I gotta go. I'll see you later."

Jasmine smiled and said, "See you later."

I made my way around the recreation center and spotted Malcolm.

"It was good beating you in checkers," I said to Malcolm.

"I don't remember everything, but I'm pretty certain you never beat me in checkers. You coming to my party?"

"I'll ask my mom." I wasn't planning on it.

Charlie said, "Don't forget that we have fart contests every day at high noon. And some impromptu ones, too. Thanks for hanging out with us old farts. You're a good kid." He slapped me on the shoulder.

I said, "Thanks. You, too."

I didn't know what that meant. I returned the shoulder slap, too. It was the wrong move. The blow knocked Charlie off course. He stumbled back into Carl, who teetered over into Malcolm, who spun and slapped Edna. I wasn't sure if he just wanted to smack Edna or if he really lost his balance.

Before I could do anything, they were all in a giant pile of old people.

"Oops," I said. I didn't know I was so powerful. Maybe hanging out there wasn't so bad...

~

PRINCIPAL BUTHAIRE MADE A POWER MOVE. He gave the teachers back their lounge and a thousand Butt Bucks to anyone who came back to school the next day. I didn't want to go, but my parents made me. I didn't know if I would actually get any Butt Bucks, but even with a thousand new ones, I was pretty certain I would still keep my title of Captain Negative.

The bell rang. Gym class was in session. We stood shoulder to shoulder down the baseline of the basketball court. It wasn't like Mr. Muscalini to be late. We waited for a few minutes before he finally walked out of the locker room. Mr. Muscalini did a double take and then stared at us, surprised.

"Oh, it's just you guys. Davenport, you looked like Grimmwolf for a second."

"I look like a seven-pound gopher?"

"Your braces remind me of when he had his. But we got him the invisible kind. He's very self-conscious sometimes."

"What are we doing for class today, Mr. Muscalini?" Randy asked.

"I don't care. Whatever you want. Or don't want. None of this means anything. I just hope Grimmwolf is safe and doesn't skip leg day. He's definitely not getting the proper amount of protein. I've never seen a gopher pound a protein shake like Grimmwolf."

"Why don't you just make a deal with Riverside to get him back?" Randy asked.

"They say they don't have him. They were just as surprised as we were. They didn't even try to take him this year."

I said, "You gotta keep hope alive, sir. Maybe he'll find his way back or they'll catch the perpetrators."

"I'm going to crush the perpetrators!"

Gulp.

Mr. Muscalini picked up a basketball, stared at it for a minute with sadness in his eyes. The sadness slowly morphed into anger. He squeezed the ball between his palms, until it exploded like a bomb went off.

He looked at me and said, "You're a good kid, Davenport. You stink at sports, but so do half of these kids."

～

I DECIDED to return Grimmwolf to Mr. Muscalini. As much as I liked not doing anything in gym class, it pained me to see him like that. Plus, I had to keep Grimmwolf a secret from Derek, which was proving problematic. I mean, how many times did a nerd like me need to go outside to the shed? The only question was how? I wasn't climbing through the ceiling and repelling down into his office again. We got lucky the first time. Nerds don't get that lucky twice in a row. I would probably end up tied up in knots with a laser in my eye.

32

As I walked through the halls on my way to science, I saw Prince Butt Hair talking to a student. He didn't look upset or about to rip out his detention pad, so at much risk to myself and my afternoons, I decided to take a closer look. I hopped from herd to herd of sixth graders until I was only about ten feet away. I was immediately concerned.

Principal Buthaire stood talking to Jasmine. I couldn't get any closer to actually hear what was being said. They were seemingly speaking just a notch above a whisper, which was also concerning. What was the big secret? If you weren't getting yelled at by Butt Hair, what was there to talk about with him?

They split up. Principal Butt Hair walked toward me. I didn't want him to see me, so I jumped into the center of the herd that had been congregating outside the sixth-grade science lab.

"Oww," some girl yelled.

"Sorry. Gotta hide from the principal."

Once Principal Buthaire had passed, I left the herd with a wave and continued on. I needed to talk to Luke. Pronto.

After science, I caught up with Luke. We walked together to the east wing.

"Dude, Jasmine was having a quiet conversation with Butt Hair before. He wasn't mad. She didn't get detention. Something fishy is going on."

"Nothing fishy is going on," Luke said defensively. "She told me about it. He wants intel on you. He's asking everybody. He wants to take you down to China Town. Whatever that means."

"What did she tell him?"

"Nothing. She said she barely knew you and that she didn't know anything you did wrong or were planning."

"Okay. Thanks. We gotta keep one step ahead of him. Maybe we should use her as a fake spy?"

"I think you're getting a little too crazy here."

"Maybe." Maybe not.

The rest of the day went as smoothly as middle school could go. There were a few farts that happened in class that I was able to avoid blame for and I had to hold my nose through the B.O. Zone outside the boys' locker room, but those were normal occurrences.

When I got back home, I had a chance to feed Grimm-wolf before Derek was done with football practice. I scooted outside while my mom was busy on the phone and opened the shed. I stepped up onto the wooden floor and looked at his cage. Oh, no! Grimmwolf was missing. As I got closer, I saw a perfect square cut out of the metal cage, gnawed through by the powerful fangs of the great gopher.

"This is bad!" I yelled to myself.

I moped back inside and texted the crew. Everyone was a bit relieved, actually. Nobody wanted me to get caught with the beast. Especially because of how the football game played out.

~

THE NEXT DAY was certainly an interesting one. As I sat with my crew checking for hair in the fourteen-bean chili, I worried about what had happened to Grimmwolf. I also wanted to count all the beans. I was pretty sure there weren't fourteen different beans in there. I was guessing two. Do fourteen different types of beans actually exist?

Anyway, I was brought back to the world with a swift elbow from my wonderful girlfriend, Sophie.

"Oww! What the heck was-" I stopped dead in my tracks as I looked up at Amanda Glusking, who stood across the table from me.

Fear surged through my body. The last time I had come in contact with Amanda was when she was sitting on my back, administering a crushing Camel Clutch on Channel 2 News that was more spine- and soul-crushing than Randy's was or could ever be. And then she finished it off with a glitter bomb to my face.

It took me a minute to realize that Jasmine had been standing next to Amanda the whole time. That's how imposing Amanda was.

"Umm, hi, Amanda."

Jasmine said, "Amanda has some ideas on what we've all been up to. I thought they could be helpful to the cause."

Amanda looked at me, fire in her eyes. "I'm tired of this Student Behavior System. It's time."

"Time for what?"

"To finish this."

I wasn't sure if I should run without even knowing what

she was talking about, but I didn't want to leave Sophie or the others behind. "Finish what?" I asked, concerned.

"Buthaire," was all she said.

"Finish him how?" I had thought about it a lot and I still didn't have any great ideas. I mean, we were wreaking havoc everywhere, but I didn't have any ideas on how to get him fired.

"The only way there is to take down a principal. Duct tape."

Even though I didn't have any better ideas, I wasn't convinced that duct tape was the only way, but I wasn't going to tell Amanda that. I didn't want to end up in the Camel Clutch again.

"But the stores will know we're coming," Sophie said. "The school was on TV with the walkout. They'll shut us down."

Amanda smirked. "I have a hundred rolls in my garage. Amazon."

"Oh, sweet," I said. "The team will discuss and we'll get back to you. Thank you. This is a great idea."

"Thanks, Amanda," Sophie said.

Amanda and Jasmine walked away, leaving our team alone to discuss the idea.

"What the heck do we do?" I asked.

Ben shrugged. "Offer her some Davenpoints and see if she does it?"

"She could probably take him down without a sweat," Sophie said.

"Then she'll take us down when she doesn't get anything for her points," I said.

"We're not getting anything for our points?" Ben asked, surprised.

"Did you really think you were going to go to space?"

"No, I hoped." Ben looked like he might cry.

Sophie said, "I think we should help her end this."

"Do you really think we can remove Butt Hair with a bunch of duct tape?" I asked.

"I think it's the only way. It took down Principal Puma. It can take down Butt Hair," Sophie said, firmly.

"She should just put him in the Camel Clutch and be done with it," I said.

"Are we really doing this?" Ben asked.

I thought for a moment. "Yep. He's going down. I'm gonna take him down to China Town."

"What does that mean?" Sophie asked.

"I'm not really sure, actually, because I don't actually want to go anywhere with him. I'm gonna go tell Amanda."

I walked over, psyching myself up in the process. Amanda and Jasmine were sitting together by the door.

I took a deep breath and said, "We're in. The crew is ready. He's most vulnerable between 2nd and 3rd period. Ms. Pierre is across the school harassing the band for being too loud, while the Peer Review Counselors are hanging out in the lounge. He'll be in the Atrium handing out detentions. We have to rush him. He's gonna know who we are. We have to have masks. He'll obviously recognize us without them, plus I think he's still using the cameras."

"We're gonna take him down to Chinatown," Amanda said, angrily.

Exactly.

33

W e had been over the plan a hundred times. It was foolproof. But I was still nervous. We were dealing with Amanda Gluskin. The human element was our only risk.

We had sent out a message on the Freedom Forum for everyone to wear black. They didn't know why, but it was so we could all blend in and not get singled out after the duct tape destruction.

We met around the corner from the Atrium in the closest empty classroom. There were three minutes left before the bell rang. We put on our masks and each grabbed a roll of duct tape. Amanda strapped on her backpack, which was basically overflowing with rolls of tape.

"Everybody ready to go?" I asked.

The Freedom Fighters nodded.

I said, "Remember, upper body first. Eliminate the hands. Cover his mouth. Then he'll be helpless."

Jasmine patted me on the back. "Nice work. This is a great plan."

"Thanks," I said. "Let's do this. We're late for Chinatown."

We sprinted out of the classroom and around the corner into the Atrium, duct tape at the ready. I spotted Butt Hair immediately. And he was in the perfect position. His back was to us as he stood in front of the Student Behavior Scoreboard. It was going to be legendary.

The crowd scattered as we approached Prince Butt Hair. I tore off my first piece of duct tape as I ran. I was about twenty feet away from the target when he turned around, a huge smile on his face. As he saw us coming, he maintained his smile. It was possible that it even widened after he saw us. My pulse quickened by about fifty times and it was already pumping at a rapid pace. I was a nerd and I was sprinting. Not a great combination.

"No!" Sophie yelled from behind me.

Red security jackets encircled me before I could get to Butt Hair. I struggled against them, but there were too many of them. And again, I was a nerd and all I had was duct tape. I was going down. Hard.

I looked around at my crew. They were being chased by various security guards around the Atrium. Other students were helping them evade capture. Amanda Gluskin was grappling with three guards and still managed to get the duct tape across Buthaire's face.

"Save yourselves!" I yelled, as I struggled against the swarm of security.

I heard a blood-curdling scream. I followed the horrible sound. Principal Buthaire lay on the ground, holding his face while Amanda Gluskin ran by me, two guards chasing her. She held a piece of duct tape with seemingly half of Prince Butt Hair's mustache attached to it. At least the mission wasn't a complete disaster. I mean, I was going to get expelled and all, and end up at LaSalle Military Academy, home for degenerate boys, but still. Sometimes, you gotta focus on the positive.

I sat in an empty classroom, guarded by two security guards. My short life flashed before my eyes. Even the sight of Principal Buthaire's patchy mustache wasn't enough to console me. I was in deep doo doo. Like the deepest doo doo you could possibly get into without ending up in prison. And I wasn't sure that was out of the question.

Principal Buthaire and Ms. Pierre stood in front of me as I sat in a student desk chair. I had never seen him so angry. Not even after I thwarted his Halloween dance takedown last year.

Butt Hair's face was beet red. A vein pulsed in his forehead as he spoke, "Your days of ruining the education of those who value their future are over."

As if things couldn't get any worse, I heard footsteps approach. My mother walked in, a look on her face that she usually reserved just for Derek and all of his stupidity.

"Please sit down, Mrs. Davenport," Principal Buthaire said. "So lovely to see you again," he said, cheerfully.

"Hello," my mother said, firmly, looking straight at me.

My mother sat down in the desk next to me. She said, "You're in a lot of trouble, misterrrrr."

Principal Buthaire looked quite pleased with himself. It made me feel worse. I was going to military school, which was bad enough, but I had finally been beaten by Butt Hair. And it didn't feel good. But how did they know it was coming? And did all my friends escape?

Ms. Pierre picked up a few papers from on top of the teacher's desk and put them in front of my mom.

I stared at the pictures, my mind racing. They were snapshots of our failed attack. They looked like they were still shots taken from a video camera.

"These were submitted to me as evidence," Ms. Pierre said.

"From whom?" my mother asked.

"They look like they're from the school video cameras," I added. "You're not supposed to use those during school hours."

My mother looked at me with lasers. That was all she needed to do to shut me up.

"Classified," was all Ms. Pierre said.

"Classified? Are you running a government agency?"

"As far as you know," Ms. Pierre said.

I didn't put it past her. I mean, I did see her do some

crazy Kung-Fu stuff to get up off the ground after the Vaseline attack. In high heels, no less.

My mother thought for a moment. "I know pretty far and I'm pretty sure this is a public school funded by my taxes and others in the community."

"As far as you know..." Principal Buthaire said.

It didn't make any sense, but most of what he said or did was in that unfortunate category.

"You're not supposed to use the cameras, as Austin said."

"It doesn't matter. I caught him red-handed with a mask and duct tape. Dozens of security guards and student eye witnesses."

"I'm going to deal with him as I see fit. You still haven't told me what supposed crime he committed? Attempted duct taping?"

Prince Butt Hair said, "He threatened me with it. Menacingly, I might add. You are fostering a culture that flouts authority. He's a floutist and I'm going to have him expelled!"

"For having duct tape in school?"

"He was wearing a mask. He was plotting to attack me with said duct tape. What if I was duct taped to the wall and didn't get my medicine? Or food or water? You could have a homicide on your hands!"

"I'm not saying he's not getting in trouble, but he didn't do anything."

Principal Buthaire's nostrils started to flare as he attempted to maintain control. He said, measuredly, "If you recall, the last middle school principal, Pushover Puma's demise came to a sticky end brought on by pompous youth and the multipurpose wonder that is duct tape. This is a serious offense which I believe you are taking too lightly. Perhaps that is the reason why his misbehaves as he does."

My mother took a deep breath. It was time for her to try to control herself. "Principal Buthaire, if my son had done this to his fifth-grade principal, I may have reacted differently. But when you turn this place into a prison and you single our son out for no good reason, I am going to fight you every step of the way."

"He broke a serious dress code rule with that mask, I'll tell you that," Principal Buthaire said, looking at Ms. Pierre for support.

Ms. Pierre stepped forward. "We are moving forward with paperwork to have Austin expelled immediately."

"Hold on one minute," my mother said, standing up. "I am not happy with what you told me about what he did or by what I saw in these pictures, but my son is not getting expelled. He's an excellent student and again, I say that he has been singled out and discriminated against by you, Principal Buthaire, from day one. Should you pursue that course of action, be prepared. I will be pursuing your firing ten times as hard."

Principal Buthaire didn't look as cocky as he did before she said that. My mother looked at me and said, "Let's go."

I was not going to argue with that one. I couldn't wait to get out of there. I glanced at Principal Buthaire and Ms. Pierre. I walked in front of my mother and led the way to the door. Both Principal Buthaire and Ms. Pierre stared at me, seemingly trying to melt my brain with their thoughts.

My mother touched my shoulder and picked off a red sticker and handed it to me.

"This was on your back," she said, handing it to me.

I took it from her and examined it. I wrinkled up my nose as I thought about it. Where would that have come from? Was it random? Was it from the security guard? Or did Jasmine Jane have some explaining to do?

34

I sat on a bean bag chair in my room, trying to keep my mind off everything that had happened and was happening. The hearing that would determine whether or not I would get expelled, which had been dubbed 'the Trial of the Century', was only a few hours away.

"How are you holding up, bud?" my dad asked.

"I don't know. I'm nervous. I don't want to get kicked out, but there's a part of me that wants this all to end. I can't take Butt Hair anymore."

"Imagine how I feel. I've had butt hair for twenty-five years."

"Funny," I said, not laughing.

"Just tell the truth and the chips will fall where they fall," my dad said.

"Those chips may fall at LaSalle Military Academy," I said, concerned.

"No, they won't. Your brother is the only one who may end up there. For you, I always thought you should go to Braddock Academy."

"Brainiac Academy?" I asked. "I guess it fits."

My dad laughed. "We'll worry about it if and when we need to. You need to own up to your mistakes. That's all you can control. That, and your attitude."

～

THE TRIAL of the Century started off with mayhem right off the bat. As I entered the auditorium with my parents, it was already filled with hundreds of people. Nervousness bubbled up inside of me. I thought it was only going to be the administration, the Board of Education, and a few friends and maybe some teachers for support. We were approaching football game attendance and it hadn't even started yet.

As people realized I had entered, they started cheering. It caught me by surprise. I wasn't expecting people to be there, let alone people cheering for me. This wasn't a Mayhem Mad Men concert or anything.

A chant started and echoed throughout the auditorium, "Free Aus-tin! Free Aus-tin!"

We headed down to the front of the room, where there was a long table with four chairs and microphones facing an even longer table with eight chairs.

My dad led the way over to a man standing in between the tables. He was tall with slicked back hair and wore a pinstriped suit. My dad shook hands with him.

"You know my wife. This is Austin. Austin, this is Mr. Willows of Willows, Stevens, Gordon, Baker, LeBlanc, Franklin, and McNulty."

Mr. Willows flashed a smile and held out his hand. "Good to meet you, Austin." He looked at my father and said, "You missed Helmsley, Charlton, and Gruber, but it was close enough."

"Sorry," my father said. He looked at me and said, "Remember, just tell the truth. Mr. Willows will be there to help you if you need it."

Mr. Willows smiled and patted me on the back. As we sat down in two of the four chairs, he leaned over and said, "We're not gonna tell the truth at all today. Sound good?"

"What are we gonna do?" I asked.

"We're going to craft a story that keeps you from getting expelled."

"Even if it isn't true?"

"That's how this works. Just follow my lead."

The administration and Board of Education filed in and sat down in the eight seats across from us. I looked around for Prince Butt Hair to make his grand entrance, but he was nowhere to be found, but then I heard boos. I followed them to see Principal Buthaire and Ms. Pierre making their way down the stairs toward the tables.

Mrs. Napolitano, our school's superintendent, tapped the microphone in front of her. "Welcome. This is certainly an interesting turnout. We are here to determine whether or not Austin Davenport will be expelled."

The crowd booed.

Mrs. Napolitano said, "I know this is an emotionally-charged situation. We will be fair and just." She looked at Principal Buthaire and said, "You've submitted the paperwork for this student to be expelled. Please state your case."

Principal Buthaire straightened his fish tie, smoothed out his still patchy mustache, and stared at me before saying, "Austin Davenport is a menace to middle school. He has racked up over a hundred detentions. He flouts authority at every turn. He defines the term floutist, in fact. I submitted a long list of infractions and suspected infractions. The straw that broke the camel's back was the latest infraction in which he attempted to attack me with duct tape."

Mrs. Napolitano's face was stone. I couldn't read her at all. She looked at Mr. Willows and said, "You are here to represent Austin?"

"Yes, ma'am."

"The floor is yours."

"Well, there is little to say other than this man here," he pointed to Principal Buthaire, "is a liar. I mean, how do you trust someone with a mustache like that? And the fish tie? It's almost criminal. Everything he said is garbage and everything my client says is the truth. And he says he's not guilty and shouldn't be expelled."

Nobody knew what to say or do. I wasn't an expert, but I was pretty certain it was some of the worst lawyering that had ever been lawyered. I looked at my parents. My mother's face was ghost white and my father's eyes were bulging out of his head. For the record, Derek was half asleep and my sister, Leighton, was texting on her phone.

Mrs. Napolitano looked at me and said, "Anything you want to say? After that, you probably should say something."

I thought for a moment. I didn't know what to say. There was so much. "Principal Buthaire is the menace. His code of conduct is seemingly harsher than prison rules and he implements those rules with extreme bias. He created a Student Behavior System that allows students to penalize other students for breaking those ridiculous rules. He is unfit to principal." I wasn't sure principal was a verb, but it sounded good.

Mrs. Napolitano looked at Principal Buthaire and he

said, "The system was all just a teachable moment to allow students to see the ills of segregation, the caste system, and the evils of a superiority mindset. It was hands-on learning."

"Objection!" Mr. Willows yelled.

"This isn't a court of law, but what is your objection?"

"He's a liar."

"Anything else?"

Dr. Dinkledorf stood up in the crowd. "Mr. Willows is correct. Principal Buthaire is a liar. If this were true, why would he not include the history department chairman to help implement such a history lesson? The truth is that Principal Buthaire is a dictator who created a system that was meant to punish students who didn't conform to his ridiculous rules."

"Thank you, Dr. Dinkledorf."

I glanced over at Principal Buthaire. He covered his brow with his hand, but I could see that his face was ruby red.

Mrs. Napolitano looked at me. "You were caught with duct tape, running toward Principal Buthaire, with a mask on, I might add. What was your intention?"

"My intention was to duct tape Principal Buthaire to the wall in an effort to bring down the flawed and discriminatory Student Behavior System once and for all."

Mr. Willows looked like he was going to puke.

The crowd broke out into pockets of surprise and chatter.

"I also spooked the dance and asked someone to fill the former teachers' lounge with rats." I looked at Zorch. "Sorry for that." I looked back at the panel. "For the record, I was only thinking of two or three rats, not twenty."

"Tell us who did it," Mrs. Napolitano said.

"I will not," I said, firmly.

"You will not?"

"You want me to rat out the kid who ratted the ratter outers?" I asked.

"I'm so confused, let's just move on. Anything else?" she asked.

"I stole Grimmwolf."

The crowd broke out into surprised chatter.

"My boy!" Mr. Muscalini burst out. "Where is he?"

"Umm, about that. He gnawed through the cage I put him in. His whereabouts are unknown."

Mr. Muscalini covered his face with his oversized hands and broke down into tears.

Ms. Pierre spoke for the first time. She said, "It is obvious by Misterrrr Davenport's own admission he's irresponsible, arrogant, and acts in a way unbecoming of a Gopher. He confessed to kidnapping. He should be expelled by his own confessions."

"It was a gopher, not a kidnapping. Had it been a baby goat, I guess we would be in a strange conundrum," I said.

The crowd chuckled. I looked at Mrs. Napolitano. Her face was still stone. I looked at the Board of Education and wasn't sure which way any of them were leaning.

Sophie stood up and yelled, "Objection, your honor!"

"This isn't a court of law, but what is it, miss?" Mrs. Napolitano said, annoyed.

"I know for a fact that he's lying."

Sophie was pointing at me. I looked behind me, but there was nobody there. Huh? How could she do this to me? My heart broke into a million pieces.

35

S ophie continued to stand, as the panel questioned her. I stared at her, not sure of what was going on. She smiled at me and then winked. I was so confused.

"And how do you know that?"

"Because I did it. All of it."

The crowd grumbled. Nobody knew what to do or say.

Except Ben. He stood up and said, "No, I did it."

And then Mr. Gifford. "No, I did it." He paused for a moment and then continued, "And there's nothing wrong with having a yellow punch buggy!"

Dr. Dinkledorf stood up slowly. "Nay, it was I who did it!"

Mrs. Funderbunk followed, "Mrs. Funderbunk did it. And don't forget to grab your tickets to the musical before they're sold out!"

Mr. Muscalini stood up and looked at me. I didn't know what he would say. He wiped a tear from his eye and said, "I did it. Except for the gopher part. I think it's pretty clear that I didn't do that."

After Mr. Muscalini was done speaking, nearly the whole room stood up, except for the panel and of course, Principal Buthaire and Ms. Pierre. I had never felt so supported in my whole life.

"Thank you, everyone. Thank you," Mrs. Napolitano said. "Please sit. We need to continue."

Principal Buthaire leaned into the microphone and said,

"I think you'll find the testimony of Derek Davenport quite interesting."

The crowd fell silent. My heart nearly stopped. I looked at my parents. Their eyes were bulging out of their heads. Nobody seemed to know anything about this.

Ms. Pierre stood up and took a seat in the front row of the auditorium, while Derek walked up onto the stage and sat down next to Principal Buthaire. I looked into the crowd. Randy, Regan, and the rest of their Peer Review idiots were laughing.

"State your name for the record."

"Derek Davenport."

"And what do you have to say?" Mrs. Napolitano asked.

"Principal Buthaire's Student Behavior System is flawed and he implements it with bias. He has told me and others on the Peer Review Committee to enforce the rules especially hard on Austin and his friends."

Principal Buthaire's upper lip was quivering. "He's biased!" he yelled into the microphone. "Austin is his brother."

"You called him as your witness," Mrs. Napolitano said.

I leaned into the microphone, "Full disclosure, my brother likes pretty much every other kid in the school more than me. He's ashamed of me because I don't have the family butt chin."

Derek said, "He's right."

The crowd really didn't know what to make of any of that.

And then the door burst open. The entire crowd turned to see who was responsible for all the commotion. It was Cheryl Van Snoogle-Something. She hustled down the stairs as the crowd continued to stare at her. Whispers and chatter spread throughout the audience.

Mrs. Napolitano stared at Cheryl, her eyebrow raised, and said, "And who might you be?"

"I'm Cheryl Van Snoogle-Something! I'm an investigative journalist for the Gopher Gazette. I have evidence to suggest Austin is innocent!"

"He's not on trial for a crime," she said, rolling her eyes. "but please enlighten us."

"I spoke to Principal Buthaire's previous two superintendents." She raised a folder in her hand. "I have an accounting of the number of detentions given before he took the job, during his tenure, and then those given by the next principal. There was a 1200% increase in detentions compared to the other principals."

"That's a lot of percent," Ditzy Dayna said.

"I thought they only went up to a hundred," Mr. Muscalini said.

Mrs. Napolitano looked at me and said, "Austin, you will not be expelled-"

The crowd went wild. It was like I was on stage with the Mayhem Mad Men at Battle of the Bands again.

Mrs. Napolitano continued, "You will reimburse the school for the rat dispos- er disbursements. And replace Grimmwolf."

"He can't be replaced!" Mr. Muscalini said.

"He's the seventh Grimmwolf we've had over the last twelve years."

"Really? What about his funeral costs?"

"He will provide a cardboard box and dig a hole behind the school," Mrs. Napolitano said, coldly.

"What about a headstone?" Mr. Muscalini asked.

"Don't get carried away."

Somebody called out, "I got the first five hundred if we can change the mascot to something more fearsome!"

"I've got a hundred for that!"

"I'll give five hundred just to upgrade to the Beavers over the Gophers!"

The Superintendent adjusted the microphone in front of her. "When we hired Principal Buthaire to lead Cherry Avenue Middle School, we were coming off of a situation where the previous principal lacked a strong disciplinarian background. Perhaps we overcompensated. Principal Buthaire, you are suspended with pay until a future course of action is charted."

The crowd jumped out of their seats and cheered. But the celebration didn't last long. In fact, it came to an abrupt end. I turned around when I heard the pitter patter of little feet running across the stage floor. Dozens of rats surged from the backstage area, heading straight for me, Principal Buthaire, and the panel.

Over the loudspeaker, a voice echoed laughter. It was a boy's voice. He spoke, "I am the Rat Man. Fear me!"

Oh, my God! It was Sal. We created a monster!

36

As soon as we got outside, I found my family, Sophie, Ben, and my other friends. They all engulfed me in a giant hug. It felt like dodgeball and I was in the Nerd Herd, tears welling up in my eyes, but they were tears of joy. I assure you that never happened during dodgeball.

After the hug broke, I looked at Derek and said, "Hey, bro. I just wanted to say thanks for what you said back there. I really believed you when you said you were ashamed of me because I didn't have the family butt chin."

"I wasn't lying," Derek said, straight faced.

"Oh."

"I didn't want you going to another school. Who would I pick on then?"

"Thanks. This is really touching."

"You want touching?" Derek grabbed me, wrapped me in a headlock, and gave me noogies. In front of my girlfriend and half the school. It was not my best moment, but I didn't care. I was staying at Cherry Avenue with my friends and Principal Buthaire was suspended and possibly getting fired.

It was a big win for the Freedom Fighters. Well, all except Jasmine Jane.

Jasmine walked over to us and stood next to Luke. I had already told him that I thought Jasmine had ratted me out to Buthaire and put the entire mission and us at risk.

"Congrats," she said. "I'm happy for you."

Even though she didn't know it would work out the way that it did, had she not ratted us out, Buthaire might still be principal. True, we probably would've had him duct taped to the wall, but who knows if that would've been the end of him. And his mustache would probably still be intact, so I was grateful that she played a role in him looking like such a doofus.

I just smiled and said, "Thanks."

~

EVEN THOUGH MS. PIERRE was still in charge of the school while Prince Butt Hair was on leave, morale was off the charts. Everyone was so pumped about the prospect of getting rid of Buthaire once and for all.

After school was over on Friday, I took my time in getting my books. I was heading over to Frank's with the crew, so I didn't have to catch the bus. We had some celebrating to do. As I walked down the hallway with Sophie and Ben, I looked up and stopped dead in my tracks. I knew the silhouette up ahead almost better than I knew Sophie's. It was Principal Butt Hair. He was holding a box in his hands. I thought about turning around, but didn't. I kind of wanted to see what he would say. And he couldn't give me detention.

"Is that Buthaire?" Ben asked.

"Yeah, and I think he's moving out. This could be huge," I said.

"Do you think he got fired?" Sophie asked.

"Here's to hoping," I said.

As we approached him, a smile spread across his dumb face. His mustache was filling in a little, but it still looked stupid.

"Misterrrr Davenport. Miss Rodriguez. Mr. Gordon. There's something you should know," he said, looking directly at me. "I always win. Even when you think you've won. You haven't. I've won."

I didn't even care. I was about to walk past him when he continued, "This whole episode you created got me a promotion. I guess I should thank you. But I won't, because I still don't like you."

The feeling was mutual. "What kind of promotion?" I asked, caring a lot more than I did a minute ago.

"I'm the new Principal of Cherry Avenue High School, home of the courageous Camels."

Wait, what? My mind was blown. "How did...How could...What?" I asked. My friends looked just as stumped as I was.

"What happened to the old principal?" Sophie managed to ask.

"He got fired. The 10th graders duct taped him to the wall or something. Lost control."

"Who is our new principal?" I asked, flabbergasted.

"I can't tell you that. It's not public knowledge, but I think you're gonna love her." Principal Buthaire laughed.

I couldn't move.

"This isn't over, Misterrrrr Davenport. I can't wait for you to get to the high school. I'll be counting the days and fine tuning the fine print on my code of conduct to thwart your degeneracy. I have a year and a half to prepare."

Then I thought about it. I didn't really care about Principal Buthaire anymore. A lot could happen in a year and a half. A lot had happened in the year and a half I had been at Cherry Avenue. I wasn't going to worry about it. He might get duct taped to the wall, too. My sister's class had taken down two principals and they had two and a half years before they graduated. It didn't seem like too many would actually graduate, but you know what I mean.

"Well, I guess we'll see you when we see you," I said.

"Let me get that door for you," Sophie said to Principal Buthaire, smiling at me.

"Be careful who you spend your time with, Ms. Rodriguez."

"I am."

We followed Principal Buthaire out the door. As Sophie

and I walked outside, a heaping rock of a man caught the corner of my eye.

I turned to see Mr. Muscalini sitting on a bench, staring up at the sky. There were tears in his eyes.

Principal Buthaire walked past him. "Don't worry, Mr. Muscalini. No need to cry. I'm only moving up to high school."

"I wasn't crying. And I wasn't crying about you. I can't stand you."

Prince Butt Hair huffed and kept going.

Mr. Muscalini wiped his tears away. He looked at us and said, "Even him leaving doesn't make me happy. There's a void in my heart that will never be unvoided."

"Mr. Muscalini. I'm sorry. I didn't want this to happen."

Sophie nudged me and pointed up the sidewalk. I turned my head to look. At first, I couldn't make out what it was that she was pointing at, but within a few seconds I could see a small ball of fur come into view on the horizon. It moved quickly toward us, bobbing up and down. What was it? I couldn't make it out.

Mr. Muscalini stood up, his eyes wide with hope. I couldn't believe it. My mouth dropped open.

It was Grimmwolf the Gopher! He trotted toward us, picking up speed as he got closer. Mr. Muscalini dropped to his knees, tears flowing down his cheeks.

"My boy! My baby boy!"

A bunch of kids exited the school as Mr. Muscalini wrapped Grimmwolf in a bear hug, nearly popping the poor gopher's eyeballs onto the sidewalk.

An eighth grader yelled, "We're back, baby! Cherry Avenue Gophers rule!"

A bunch of football players called out, "Woof! Woof!"

Based on my time spent with Grimmwolf, that was a

gross exaggeration of what a gopher sounded like. It was more like a chirping bird than a junkyard dog, but I didn't want to rain on their parade. Their beloved lucky charm had returned. The Cherry Avenue Gophers would be a force to be reckoned with come next fall.

And then I nearly jumped out of my skin as Mr. Muscalini screamed.

"Ahh! I taught you better than that!" Mr. Muscalini shook out his fingers.

I held in a laugh. Grimmwolf was definitely a biter.

Bobby Newman walked over to me and said, "Nice work, Davenport. My party tomorrow night is in your honor."

When he said the word honor, I thought of the Honor Society and the crew at the VRC.

"It's tomorrow at 3 P.M."

"Why does that sound familiar?" I asked Sophie.

"Because that's when Malcolm's birthday party is."

I looked at Bobby and said, "Thanks for the party and all, but I have somewhere I gotta be."

"We're celebrating the end of Butt Hair, dude! I'm calling it, Bon Voyage, Butt Hair! It's gonna be epic."

"I know," I didn't want to break it to him that Butt Hair was going to the high school. "but I gotta break a few old men out of a retirement home."

Bobby looked at me sideways. "Okay...You're a strange dude, Davenport."

"Thanks," I said, walking away with Sophie and Ben.

~

IT WAS a little after 3 P.M. on Saturday afternoon. I walked into Vintage Retirement Community with Sophie and Ben, carrying a takeout bag from Burger Boys. Malcolm couldn't eat steak, but Burger Boys had one of the best ground steak burgers around, so I figured it would make him happy. We also had ten tickets to the Bear Creek Barn Burners, an independent baseball team. Bear Creek didn't have a Starbuck's but they had baseball. My dad got tickets from work. We were going to take the VRC crew to a game come spring time.

We walked into the recreation room and I couldn't believe it. It was mayhem. And I hadn't caused it.

Randy was under a pile of old people, struggling to get free. Malcolm, Carl, Charlie, and Ethel sat on top of him.

"You cheater!" Malcolm yelled.

Carl said, "It ain't high noon, Charlie, but how about a fartin' contest?"

"I'm way ahead of ya. I'm three farts in!"

Randy groaned as he continued to struggle. Ethel was sitting on his back while Malcolm started biting Randy's leg.

"Give him the Camel Clutch, Ethel!" Charlie yelled.

"Malcolm, are you sucking on my leg?" Randy asked, disgusted.

"I'm biting you, but I don't have my dentures in!"

Malcolm looked up at me and said, "Alvin, can you help me find my dentures?"

Aahh farts...

COMING SOON!

NEW RELEASE ON 2/14/2020
(VALENTINE'S DAY- DUH...)

4/15/2020

6/15/2020

Got Audio?

Want to listen to Middle School Mayhem?

ABOUT THE AUTHOR

C.T. Walsh is the author of the Middle School Mayhem Series, set to be a total twelve hilarious adventures of Austin Davenport and his friends.

Besides writing fun, snarky humor and the occasionally-frequent fart joke, C.T. loves spending time with his family, coaching his kids' various sports, and successfully turning seemingly unsandwichable things into spectacular sandwiches, while also claiming that he never eats carbs. He assures you, it's not easy to do. C.T. knows what you're thinking: this guy sounds complex, a little bit mysterious, and maybe even dashingly handsome, if you haven't been to the optometrist in a while. And you might be right.

C.T. finds it weird to write about himself in the third person, so he is going to stop doing that now.

You can learn more about C.T. (oops) at ctwalsh.fun

 instagram.com/ctwalshauthor
facebook.com/ctwalshauthor

ALSO BY C.T. WALSH

Down with the Dance: Book One

Santukkah!: Book Two

The Science (Un)Fair: Book Three

Battle of the Bands: Book Four

Medieval Mayhem: Book Five

Future Release schedule

Valentine's Duh: February 14th, 2020

The Comic Con: April 15th, 2020

Election Misdirection: June 15th, 2020

Education: Domestication: August 15th, 2020

Class Tricked: September 15th, 2020

Graduation Detonation: November 15th, 2020

Made in the USA
Monee, IL
12 November 2020